BORN TO SERVE

The Diary Of A Female Bartender

Desmond Drue

ISBN: 0985746254
ISBH-13: 9780985746254
Library of Congress Control Number: XXXXX (If applicable)
LCCN Imprint Name: City and State (if applicable)

BORN TO SERVE

I have a disturbing sense of self
'Oh miss, on the rocks please. I pour through drinks
In an endless pursuit of what ails them;
Some I know,
Others refrain from familiarity,
They drink from the altar
Of what keeps them up at night.

CONTENTS

REAL OR MEMOREX

"Unbutton it."

"Unbutton it, my ass."

"If you don't unbutton it, you're not working tonight."

"Fuck, Buster. it's unbuttoned. It's not supposed to be open down to my navel."

"What?"

"I said this ain't the Yellow Banana on Route One."

"They're fake huh?"

"They ain't fake Buster. They're as real as they get."

"Sure, Nora"

"Wouldn't you like to know?"

"Well, I know one thing. The male patrons want to check you out. You know damn well, the more cleavage, the more drinks. The more drinks, the more tips."

"Damn it, Buster. What kind of talk is that? A girl's got to leave a little to the imagination. You think this is easy, standing behind this bar, serving these juice heads all night. Them gawking, like thirsty men in the desert. I give enough of myself here. There's just some things, I just ain't giving up, like surrendering all sense of propriety."

"Like showing your boobs?"

"Yeah, to begin with."

"Shit, Nora, you're a damn bartender, not a nun."

"Just drop it, Buster. Will yeah?"

"OK Just a few damn buttons, Nora. Get it?"

1

Desmond Drue

"O.k., ok, will do, but you are going to get yours someday. Mark my words, the ignorant asshole that you are."

I had been working for Buster, the manager at four months. He was a imbecile. I wished I could soften up on him but it wasn't my nature. Buster was just full of himself. He was a person who extracted a little power, not a lot but rather a tad, and it had blown his head way out of proportion. He walked around the restaurant like he was king of an empire. He managed the bar like it was his own fiefdom. He was so full of himself that he was hard to reason with. He only has one point of view, and it being his, it circumvented all others. He had no empathy for the other eight billion people in the world.

My demeanor changed immediately upon seeing him. I went from being a rather socially engaged woman in my mid-twenties to a closed down anti-social one who could hardly utter a few words (Well that was in his presence). In his absence I spoke my twenty-one thousand a day, the average spoken by most American woman.) We American women speak a lot because we have a lot to say.

I couldn't help looking at Buster with disgust. I have tried to search out his good attributes, (because I am a Christian) but honestly, after months of trying I just said ,"screw it". I was no shrink, no social worker, or life coach. I was just a normal girl trying to make a living.

"Nora, get back to work."

"Nora, get back to work." What's that all about? All I do is work. I can't believe the fat unkempt degenerate is laying a guilt trip on me. I didn't know why I was surprised? When he hired me at McGlynn's, he laid it out as plain as he could I remembered it loud and clear.

"I'm going to be upfront with you Nora. It is what it is and I'm going to say it as I see it. I don't think you're the smartest turnip on the truck and better put, your elevator doesn't go up to the top floor but there's something I like about you. You're good looking, I only hire good looking girls, and you have a nice set of boobs. Real or not but it's obvious you have a good set and parade them around masterfully. Some girls don't know what they got and others use it like it was paramount to who they are. You got a damn good skill set and you damn well know that they're your moneymakers. That's what they are and you are wise to use them. God didn't give them to you for nothing you know. With all this shit being said, you're hired."

"*What a scumbag*", I said to myself. "*What a low life, scum of the earth piece of crap.*" I had all I could do to keep from vomiting. "*This is going to be a shit experience at best*", I remembered myself saying. "*My elevator might not go to the top floor, but I know it goes stories higher than this shit bag could ever ascend, being there is no doubt in my mind the low life lives in a cesspool*".

"So you're probably asking yourself, "Then why did she take the job?"

I took the job because I was as poor as a church mouse. I couldn't get much poorer. It was all because of the bad decisions I made. Everyone has a story to tell, and there sure is a lot of misery to go around, but I felt most people learned from their mistakes (do they?) but not me Nora Bergman. I learned nothing from my past other than I was driven to repeat it, and honestly I hadn't a clue why. But if there is a germ of my demise. I guess I can start with my two ex-boyfriends, Marc and Trevor, although there were many others. Most were "bad boys" and being who they were attracted me like a bee to honey. As Buster had a habit of saying "It is what it is", probably the smartest words that ever came out of his mouth. Yes, no choir boys for me, no goody two shoes, no polite gentle momma's boy. I wanted my men sassy and hard, the harder, the better I liked it (but I did draw a line). There were some bad boys who scared the stuffing out of me. I guess I wanted them bad but manageable.

Did you ever hold a lit match that burned your skin? You held onto to it until the sanity in you said, "let the damn thing go" but you held on and suffered the consequences nonetheless, asking why? Unfortunately, I was one of those who would hold onto it until my flesh was burnt to the bone. I must had have some kind of insane attraction to pain because in my world, it was at the center and there never seemed to be any salve or release to diminish the residual effect. It kept on hurting and there was absolutely no way for it to heal, being as I could not distance myself from the attraction. So like a fly which is attracted to light, I was attracted to my "bad boys" and was singed time and time again, although looking at me, most people would say I wore the pain well.

If I was anything, I was a survivor. I really didn't think I had any survival skills, but surprise, surprise, I had more than I could count. I amazed myself that I could pull myself up by my proverbial "bootstraps" after I was beaten down. I was unaware that I had all these resources locked up inside me, ready to come to my rescue when needed and called upon, more than a few times, dozens, if not hundreds, as I looked back on my less than stellar life.

I am a Bergman, a Germantown Bergman. In Swedish *berg* means "mountain" and *man*, as in English" means "man". In both my and my mother's case it was a misnomer. Our name should have been Bergwoman, because we indeed were the mountains of strength in our family. It was in our female genes that for whatever reason, we had the uncanny ability to carry water on both shoulders. My mother somehow passed it to me in a way I was unaware of, which was not shared with the rest of my siblings. They mostly took after my father, a gentle soul who swam in calm waters . My mother on the other hand was a force to be reckoned with. In a confrontation with her, there was always one clear winner and it was Linnea Bergman. Her waters were choppy and deep, surrounded by icebergs, mountains of ice.

I was born in Viroqua Wisconsin, population 4,362, the poorest town in the state. It was probably one of the coldest places in the world for three or four months of the year but one of the most beautiful for four as well. As for the remaining, they were kind of in limbo. They could lean one way or the other, supporting the cool but clear crisp winds coming off the lakes or reinforcing the winters that Wisconsin was known for, unrelenting, unforgiving, making its population, mostly Swedes, Germans and Norwegians the sturdiest of stock.

I was born to Nicolas and Linnea Bergman in 1989. My father was kindred of calm, standing six feet and weighting a hefty two hundred fifty-three pounds he gave a diametrically opposite impression of who he really was. I was told at a young age what you see is not always what you get and that being said, the world is full of surprises. As I grew older, I found that statement to be not only true but also one of life's absolutes. If one did not know my father, his presence alone commanded respect. His size along with his natural gait gave him a greater presence than he ever asked for. Quiet by nature he liked his solitary moments, or to be surrounded by his five children, of which I was the antsy third to be born. My father provided me with a desire to find that peace I felt he had captured within, thereby freeing himself from all the frivolous desires most men seek. What my father held was perspective, allowing incredible peace of mind built on not wanting anything material but only that which was free, and not having him to support the mundane. His free moments had a value that in their simplest form indeed held the treasures in his life. My father took nothing for granted, and loved nature and its ever-changing landscape, but not as much as he loved his children and watching them grow.

What I learned from my father was to surround myself with things that have worth, to keep a clear mind and to live an uncluttered life. To never give all of myself away, but to always save something that would only be mine and expand upon it each and everyday. My father taught me to be as clean as the new fallen snow, to be as pure as the icy north wind, to be one with nature and the people I love, to never serve anything up with a mean spirited heart. To find God and speak to Him/Her, during my weakest and strongest moments, speak to God because He/She exists in one form or another, and He/She might be listening. My father was a Catholic but never went to church. He found the altar of God in the soft, warm breeze of a summer's day, the airy unpredictability of a threatening winter sky, the unstructured concert of his children's voices. My father in life and spirit was all in. If he saw me now, he would be mortified.

My mother's name was Linnea. Standing a mere five fee, and she was a contradiction in terms. As quiet as my father was, my mother was precise and powerfully spoken and was known to rattle the dishes in our kitchen cabinets when she raised her voice to make a point. She was the frontline of defense against the world. My father had an innate ability to be selectively inattentive. He didn't want to see what he didn't want to see. He didn't want to be engaged in anything that rocked his sled off course. When my father saw true north, he was headed there. He was almost impossible to dissuade him. My mother, on the other hand, looked for every dip in the road, every pit in the pie. If there was a wrong to be righted, it was her crusade. If a word was out of sync with the spirit of the moment, she would take issue.

My mother saw herself as a crusader, with the ample desire and full ability to change, that, which exists, to disassemble all the parts of the universe and to put them in a different order. She empowered herself by her inarguable stance, that the world (basically everywhere she looked) was full of itself and was going haywire. She saw it distinctly as needing a change for the better and her desire was not to change it for herself, because, as she stated a thousand times, Your father and I have seen the best of times, and although we don't have all the stuff that makes other people take notice, what we do have, goes beyond the cover of any book. It has core and value, anything people have beyond that, is just for show, Nora, just for show ."

My mother, like most women, dedicated her life to her children, She knew she and my father would never get out of Viroqua, the truth is they had no desire. They were very comfortable in their functionality. Dad going to work everyday cutting timber at the local mill. Routinely doing what he did and never looking beyond it, and my mother forever looking for a cause, or a battle to fight as she determinedly set about on her mission, as evangelist.

"It's all about you kids" she would constantly say to us. "The truth is someday, probably sooner than you think, me and Dad will be gone. You can't live forever you know, and you five had better be able to fend for yourselves. It's you I worry about the most, Nora. You might be the middle child, probably the safest place a child can be in a family but you got an antsy-ness about you that sometimes scares the hell out of me. There's something in you that is unsettling. I can't quite wrap my arms around it but it's there and really apparent, to those who take a moment to notice and that's everyone now. You being such a pretty young thing, you draw attention like a magnet does to iron."

My mother was damn right. I was an antsy child, unlike my brothers Viktor and Samuel, and my sisters, Elin and Hannah, who very much seemed to blend in with the local flavor. I felt I was suffocating, and about to drown. The thought of getting married and knocking out a bunch of kids and being confined within a small town mentality was beyond my imagination.

The only way I felt I could escape the predictability of my future was to go to college, join the Army or just pick up my belongings (the few I had) and just leave. The truth was I wasn't college material, I could have been if I'd applied myself, but for whatever reason, I had no desire. School to me was just a boring dead-end place that molded everyone to its complete sameness. Even if I had wanted to go to college, my family didn't have the means to send me there and if they had, it would have gone to Elin and Viktor, seemingly the smartest, and most hardworking of my siblings.

The thought of entering the military, did cross my mind at times. The army now was opening its ranks to more women and I occasionally fantasized about being in the midst of all those young horny soldiers. But I concluded eventually that, I wasn't cut out for fatigues and combat boots. The only real option and the one finally capturing my determination was I just had to get out of Viroqua, *but to where?*

I now found myself as a young woman torn between two different mentalities. The gentle, almost surrealistic one of my father telling me to be one with the earth and not to let the turbulence and the influences of the mundane world get the better of me and the aggressive, take no prisoners one of my mother, who lived her life on the edge, causing mayhem where ever she went, destroying the norm as it crossed her path, always looking for the fly in the ointment and never happy until she found it.

I wanted so very much to be like my father, God's gentlest soul, at peace in a disconcerting way. (How he achieved it with my mother around was a miracle unto itself.) I prayed, as my father suggested, that I would wake up someday feeling as he did (my life would have been so much easier) but I did not. I woke up as the child of my mother, full of angst and rage, befuddled and angry that the world was as it was. A bastion of unpredictability, restlessness, crying out in the darkness. I wanted more. I wanted more. I wanted more!

VIKING, OR NO VIKING

I was now twenty-two years old and had been dating Hans, for nearly three years. He was a handsome boy, tall and muscular with a swath of gold hair. He looked like he was a pureblood Viking and treated me so well all the girls at Laurel High were smitten with envy. I loved it. This was the part of me that sometimes reared its ugly head : unsettling, the one-upmanship, making me want to be better than everyone else. Wanting to pay the world back, but for what. My relationship with Hans was seemingly a match made in heaven. Me, with my blond hair and large hazel eyes and a body that made men and boys swoon, I was the perfect complement to him. The sex although not as frequent as I would have desired was a cut above the rest or at least I fantasied it was, hoping it would bring me to a deeper understanding and appreciation for Hans. It did not. Although I slept with several other older boys, I drew the conclusion, that the sex with Hans, just mirrored what continued life would be with him, mundane, boring, uninspired, at best . There would be an ordinariness about it that scared me senseless. It would be lock-stepped and I wanted more out of life, so much more!

The truth is, I had already gone beyond Hans. He was now a part of my past, but not of my future'. There was no excitement in our relationship. I was bored with

Viroqua and found absolutely no reason to stay other than my family, which disappointingly, I felt was breaking away from its core, as my siblings grew older and were captured by their own interests.

I knew it was time for me to leave. I questioned myself: *"What would keep me here?"* Not Hans. In a nonchalant way, I felt he could be easily replaced. Not Viroqua, Wisconsin. It was just too small for me. I wanted bigger. I wanted more.

Unfortunately, not my family. Although at one time as close as it could be, it was not as it was. Different ages fractured it, with different beliefs, different wants and desires, different fates.

My family was my last bastion of hope to keep me tethered to the anchor of my small community My family, my family. my family. I decided to leave it behind. It was holding me back. I would not let it be my family curse

BOSTON BOUND

Would it be L.A or Boston? I was drawn by both coasts but didn't know about these two cities other than what I researched. There were plus and minuses to both.

Both had main attractions that were active, outdoor places. Being a Wisconsin girl, I damn well spent most of my time outdoors. Known for its fifteen thousand lakes and flat marshes, Wisconsin was an outdoor paradise. There was no way I would ever go to a place that didn't have an enthusiastic outdoor offering. Both Boston and L.A. provided such an attraction. Boston had its common and public gardens, the esplanade, the Freedom Trail, Castle Island, Arnold Arboretum and accessible green spaces all over.

L.A. was also an outdoor person's destination. A vibrant city, it was surrounded by some of the most beautiful beaches in the world. The water accessibility and sporting were unlimited. This coupled with an abundance of rolling hills and mountains, provided a perfect palette for rock climbing and sky diving, activities I had never tried, but was very willing to explore.

L.A.'s weather was beautiful all the time. I had mixed emotions about this. A part of me loved the idea of discarding my winter clothes, and scaling back my closet to my summer's best but then there was another side of me, telling me I would become insanely bored with beautiful skies and temperatures in the high seventies to mid-eighties forever. I was used to seasonal change and honestly looked forward to wearing a sweater when summer hinted of fall, or a parka when winter blew its first chilling wind. I concluded I was addicted to the seasons and their passing without my experiencing them, caused within me a slight tremor.

I also wanted a vibrant city only youth could support. I couldn't see myself anywhere there was an abundance of old people. The majority of Florida cities I ruled out, although I did some research on Miami. It caught my interest for a while but quickly faded because, frankly, it seemed way too fast for me. I still considered myself a small town girl and thinking about moving to L.A. or Boston, was a real stretch, but Miami was, as I decided, beyond my scope.

The average age in Boston was in the late thirties. In L.A. it was about thirty-four years. I was in my early twenties. The average age in Viroqua was in the mid forties. Even though, the population was older, because of its addiction to outdoor activity made it seem much younger. I never thought really old people surrounded me. The problem? I was surrounded by old ideas.

The reality check for me was that I was told Viroqua was rather cheap to live in, with a family income of $24,406, as opposed to Boston at $72,907 and L.A. at $55,809. For the past few years, I had been holding down a part-time secretarial job paying me $11, 438 a year. I was just twenty-two but having no college degree, I could not envision me having any future. The reality was that I envisioned myself going nowhere. The more I thought about my future, the more determined I was to get out of Viroqua.

Viroqua was a dead-end street. I wanted so much more. How I was going to survive in either Boston or

L.A? I hadn't a clue, but how I was going to survive in Viroqua Village I knew I hadn't a glimmer of hope. It would be either Boston or L.A. Either would provide me the lifeline I needed to better my life or it would be me constant spiraling into a dark abyss.

Another factor played a significant role. One obsession I always had is sports. This is why I eventually chose Boston. I was a Wisconsin cheese-head from the day I was born. Viroqua offered high school and college football on Saturday afternoons. And then there were the legendary Green Bay Packers on Sunday. Life without the Wesby High School Norsemen and the Wisconsin Badgers but most importantly , the great, awesome, incomparable, legendary Green Bay Packers, was unthinkable. For me to exist in a secondary football market or in a state or city that didn't have an insatiable football appetite was unfathomable.

I loved the Packers. I knew I could grow to love the Patriots; the team the rest of America (except the majority of New Englanders) loved to hate. What was not to love? The Patriots were winners and I damn well knew why the people of Boston and the surrounding areas identified with them. Because there is an adrenaline rush in supporting a winner, a team you feel never lets you down, seldom takes the legs out from under you. That is always in every game and never lies down for its opponents.. The Pats are winners. Winners. And I damn well wanted to be a winner too.

I decided to go to Boston. Nothing now would deter me. How I would get there I didn't know. How I would tell my family and my boyfriend Hans, I hadn't a clue. I wasn't very skilled at looking for work or applying for a job, but I decided I had better bone up and learn fast because there was just no turning back now. I was on a fast track, leaving my small town life behind, and it would be nothing but the big stage for me. Hurray, hallelujah, hurray, hurray, hurray. I'm Boston bound, I'm Boston bound. Damn it. Boston bound.

A YOUNG BIRD
FROM IT'S NEST

It was difficult telling my parents and siblings I was leaving Viroqua. My siblings reinforced that I would be going out into a world that was way too big for me. I told them that the smallness of our community was swallowing me up alive.

My father was very emotional. He didn't want to see any of his offspring leave the nest. His life was happiest when his children were within ear and eyeshot. He loved the comfort of them being around and the fear of them in the unknown paralyzed him.

"I really wish you would reconsider. The world out there is a lonely and scary place. It's really no place for a single gal, from a small town to be?"

"I understand Daddy. It's not that I'm leaving our family. I mean, I'm a Bergman and forever will be a Bergman. It's not that I'll never return. You'll see me often enough, I mean, we'll enjoy the holidays together and such."

"Well, life won't be the same without you."

"Daddy, you'll have all the other kids to contend with. My God, the four of them alone are a handful, and then there's Mom."

My father didn't say a word. He knew what I meant.

My mother got it. Like most things, she had a handle on me wanting to get out of Viroqua. She had looked long and deeply at the community as a whole and the individuals who comprised it. Then after peeling back the onion, she came to conclude there was enough dirt and bad interest in the people of Viroqua, that staying in the town or leaving, wouldn't make a hell of a lot of difference.

"Viroqua has got its own kind of disease. Just because it's a small town, doesn't discount one damn bit there is a cancer growing in side it. Small town people do small town things but every now and again, one of our community members takes one giant big bite of that juicy forbidden apple and the shit sure enough hits the fan.

I heeded my Mother's every word. But, damn it, nothing that she could ever say, now could deter me, My mind became more determined, as I listened on. She was consistent with being Mother Bergman, driving her children to be the best they can, supporting their every quest to break through their demons.

"Nora, you're just as exposed here, as you would be anywhere else. There are bad people in Viroqua and you and I damn well know who they are. In fact, I will tell you, all the town folk knows who they are. And they have kindred everywhere. Yes, they do. They have bad brothers and sisters all over the place, and you can damn well bet they have them in Boston too. No, Boston isn't immune. Therefore, I guess, I guess what I'm saying is if you need to go, then you need to go. You damn well have my blessing. But be damn careful. There's vermin and scum everywhere. They're all around us. Now, a dumb person doesn't know that, and I damn well didn't raise no dumb daughter. Did I?"

"No, no, Mother. No you didn't", I replied.

"Then that's it. Go with your mother's blessing. Boston. I know nothing about it other than them, Boston baked beans."

DON'T BITE THE HANS THAT NEEDS YOU?

My boyfriend Hans was crushed. He couldn't believe what he was hearing. Unbeknown to me, he had big plans for us, plans he had never discussed with me. Now I told him our relationship wasn't good. It was o.k., but o.k just didn't really have the glue to hold me to it, and as I prioritized my reasons for staying (which truthfully came down to a pitiful three), he didn't even make the short list.

"But Nora I had it all worked out."

"Worked out,?" I questioned in disbelief.

"Yeah, like I had it all planned. Every bit of it."

"Every bit of it. You mean like every detail? I mean, like those you never shared with me?"

"Yes, those."

Sometimes, I thought that Hans was just feeble of mind.

"Like, don't keep me in suspense. Like, I communicated to you what my plans were. I'd like to hear how you incorporated me into yours."

Hans was as meek as could be.

"Well, I love you Nora. You know I love you and have hoped you love me in return and we could continue on as we have for a few more years, then get married and have kids.

I couldn't believe what I was hearing, that Hans `loved me. He never spoke of that emotion, not even once. It was something we didn't share. "How the hell could he say he loves me? We're both were wet behind the ears. Newbies to this whole "love" thing. I bet I was the first girlfriend he ever had. It must be the sex. He dipped his pen in my ink, and he damn well confused it with love. He hasn't a clue, and the truth be known, neither do I. And getting married? He must be insane. I would never entertain marrying him and the idea of me having babies with him would drive me to do the most desperate of things. It was way beyond my ability to comprehend. I realized for the first time (my head must have been buried in the sand) that the only reason I was with him for three years is that I was just too lazy to break from him. I listened like a dog would to its master. Every word coming out of his mouth was bullshit. I let him dribble on, letting one word after another trip over itself in a rare exhibition of dumb foolery. He was making an ass out of himself, but it was so damn entertaining in such a pathetic way, I let him dribble on.

"I love you Nora, with my whole heart and soul."

I didn't say a word but answered him in my head.

"Bullshit, Bullshit, Bullshit. I should really take him over my knee and spank him."

I love you more than I have ever loved anyone ever in my life."

"What a pathetic asshole. I can't believe what he is spewing. It's making me nauseous. I don't feel well. I'm about to puke."

19

Then the whole episode turned worse, beyond melodramatic. The wimp started to cry. I could carry the burden of a lot of things, but to see a six foot hunk of man lay a fountain of tears on me, it was just too much for me to take. Hans didn't need a girlfriend; he needed a wet nurse. I wanted to cut his balls off right there, laying this shit on me like I needed to hear it. Hans just could not man up. He was no way prepared for the real world and that's just the reason I wanted to leave Viroqua, because I myself was drowning in it's blight.

What I hated about meeting with Hans, was he never asked one question about me, never about the emotions I held, never about the reasons I felt so compelled to leave. Not one question was asked, not a pry about how difficult it would be to leave my siblings and parents. Not one. Not one. Not one. It was all about him. It was all about him. I wanted to scream at the top of my lungs. "It's all about you, you self-absorbed man child disappointment!"

It was over between us. I couldn't take much more of this. There was a time when I thought we might somehow maintain a friendship and possibly more. That was gone as quickly as a carton of Kleenex in a woman's bathroom. My emotional box was empty. I wanted to relieve this poor pathetic creature of his misery, like the Viking heritage to which he was linked. I wanted to take my father's antique sword (the Viking traditional Ulfberht) and cut out Hans heart, but I gently planted a token kiss on his rosy cherub cheeks. Goodbye, you sorry ass man-child.

BETTY

"Call me Betty. Going to Boston?"

"Yup, to start a new life, kind of an adventure." I answered.

"Really, it takes a lot of courage to venture out alone. I've been alone since my husband passed several years back. It's a scary place when you're just one. Aren't you afraid?"

At that very moment, I wasn't but as I moved closer to Boston, I couldn't say I wasn't feeling anxious.

"Honestly, yes, frightened but excited. Gonn'a get myself a job, an apartment of my own, discover what Boston has to offer, the gardens, North End, the Charles, the art museum, find me some new friends, and oh, yes, follow the great New England Patriots. Second to the Green Bay Packers, the best football team ever."

"Wow, you really seem excited."

"Breaking from Viroqua and family tradition is a really big deal."

Betty, very compassionately, replied "Well, young lady, I don't mean to pry but let me give you a little motherly advice. Boston ain' no Viroqua, Wisconsin. It ain't no small village. It's every bit as exciting and scary as you say, especially if it's your first encounter with the big city and you being young and alone."

I pushed back at her. I felt empowered. "I'm ready for it. It's my time. Sometimes, you just know what's right and right now Boston is right for me. Why are you traveling?"

"Coming from Germantown to visit my son and his family They live in Westwood. Like I said, it's really scary when you don't have anyone, being my husband passed several years back. His dying has been the biggest loss of my life. You damn well don't know what you have until you lose it. Unfortunately, my life will never be the same."

Five hours later, we were arriving at the Greyhound terminal, 700 Atlantic Avenue, Boston, Massachusetts. Betty and I shook hands and wished each other well.

"Nice talking with you. I hope you have a lovely visit with your son and his family."

"Yes, thank you. It was nice talking to you as well. Now, remember what I said, being one who seldom offers any advice. Boston is no Viroqua. It isn't Viroqua. It isn't a small Midwest village. Be careful, stand tall and strong, and buy a pair of combat boots and hope you don't have to use them."

CLUELESS

Whatever possessed me? I must have been insane. I couldn't believe I had made this decision and how it weighed upon me at this very moment. It was like a thousand-pound piece of granite on my chest, stripping me of my ability to catch my breath. I was gasping for air. I was now hyperventilating. I was in a 100 percent panic attack. I was scared beyond belief.

"Are you o.k. Miss?"

It was like I couldn't comprehend who was speaking to me.

"Miss, are you alright?"

My blurry vision was now coming back. I turned and looked at the bus driver who showed considerable alarm.

"Miss, do you need a hand to get off the bus? All the other passengers have exited but you, and your suitcase is sitting on the curb."

"Yes, yes. I mean no, no. I'm fine. I can get off the bus on my own accord."

"Fine miss. Then I'll just step aside."

The driver took two steps back towards the seat, and I took three steps down off the bus and walked towards my one bag, looking as lonely as I felt. I hadn't a clue where I was now going or what I was going to do. It had taken all my energy to get me from Viroqua to Boston, and as absurd as it seems, I never really thought about what I was going to do once I got here.

It had taken seventeen hours and cost me one-hundred and eight dollars for the one-way fare. I now had two thousand and sixty-three dollars left, which would be a rich man's ransom in Viroqua but was significantly less meaningful in a big city like Boston.

I grasped onto my bag, and on the verge of tears I made a beeline to Starbucks across the street from the bus station. I needed a place to sit for a spell, a place to think, a cup of hot coffee to recharge my battery, and to put on my thinking cap. I purchased a cup of hot roasted and sat on a stool, observing the pedestrians walking by at a hurried pace. I thought there was more people and activity on this one corner than there was in my entire hometown.

I finished the coffee but was still in a quandary. What would I do? No, no, what would Linnea do? Yes, what would my Mother do alone in the city, if she was a young girl like me? I needed to go somewhere safe. Yes, that is what Linnea would do. And that meant the YWCA, the Young Women's Christian Association. They sure would have an open room for me.

I took a cab to the YWCA, at 140 Clarendon Street. It was an old building that somehow greeted me with a welcoming face. I walked up to the older woman at the front desk and told her my plight. She was in her late fifties, with a wrinkled but pleasant face. The characteristic that most struck me was her gentle soft hazel eyes falling like those of an old basset hound. She listened most attentively to my plight and with an easiness so as not to install any more anxiety she spoke.

"Nora, is it?"

"Yes, Nora it is."

"Well, my dear, I'm sorry to say, the YWCA is not the organization it was years back, having the flexibility and pray tell, the financial resources to provide an absolute menu of services."

I didn't know what she was trying to tell me but I listened anyway.

"What I'm trying to say is that, unlike prior years when we would have a rather large number of rooms available to shelter needy women, today it's not the case. Frankly, we don't have the financial wherewithal to do it."

I was getting very tired and more frustrated by the moment. I didn't need any long-winded explanation. I just needed a damn room. I spoke up abruptly.

"Do you have a room or don't you?"

"Well miss, the answer is, no, we don't."

"Well, then, it's been one long day, I'm getting out of here."

I quickly thanked her and then took several steps towards the door.

"How many days do you think that you might need a room.?" the woman asked. I turned around, and dragging my suitcase behind me, took six steps towards her.

"I don't really know. I just got into town and I'll start looking for a job tomorrow. Honestly, I'm not quite prepared for my stay in Boston. I think as they say in my hometown, "I'm befiddled and befuddled.""

"How quaint?"

"We'll I guess I was in too much of a hurry to get out of Viroqua."

"Viroqua?"

"Viroqua, Wisconsin."

"Well, I don't mean to pry, but what are you going to do now?"

The question elicited a tear. I hadn't a clue.

"I don't know. I really don't know what to do."

"Well, then, let me introduce myself. My name's Sylvia Brie ."

"Like the cheese?"

"Yes, like the cheese. It seems we do have some-thing in common, you being from Wisconsin, the cheese capital of the world and all."

"Well, It's great we met, but it's really not helping me find a place to sleep tonight."

Ms. Brie walked around her desk and towards me.

"Well, I have a suggestion. I live alone and you seem like a very nice young lady. And certainly one under duress, so it seems."

I interrupted and spoke anxiously. "Yes Ms. Brie."

"Sylvia. If you please."

"Sylvia, I know it seems that I'm under a lot of duress, because I am."

"We'll, that being said, why don't you consider spending the night at my apartment? And perhaps you might stay a bit until you find a place to live. And you said that you don't have a job. Well, until you find your-self employed."

I had no choice but to say yes.

"And if you like the situation, meaning it works out for the both of us, then I'll charge you a small token rent, say fifty dollars a week. What do you say to that?"

I just couldn't do better than this.

"Fifty dollars a week. It's a deal."

I knew I must have looked like a homeless puppy being let in from the cold. I was.

"Well, then Nora," Sylvia reached out to shake my hand. I extended my hand as well and we shook, "Then it's a deal. We'll see how it works out. I have a feeling this will be great for the both of us. I'll be leaving for home in about thirty minutes. Why don't you sit over there on the chair and rest for a bit."

Rest, I could have fallen asleep and slept on the floor. I was beyond exhaustion. But I was in Boston. The home of Boston baked beans, the New England Patriots and my new life.

ROSIE, MY ARCH ANGEL

"Pay attention."

"I am."

I really wasn't. I couldn't keep my eyes off him. Randy was one of the servers. We were both new hirers at the Cheddar house, a new restaurant and bar in the North End. I was hired as a bartender. I had never tended bar in my life. When the manager Jason asked me, if I had experience, I lied. I damn well knew, he knew I didn't. Why he hired me, with so many experienced bartenders in Boston, I hadn't a clue but one thing clearly resonated. His interest in me went beyond work. He kept staring at me in the strangest way. It caused me goose bumps and made me shiver.

The Cheddar House was to open in just a few days. Many of the employees were less than excited.

"I can't see this joint making it" Caroline the hostess constantly murmured under her breathe. "It's a damn beer and burger house in the North End. People don't come down here for filler food. They come here for Italian food, the best damn Italian food in the whole United States in fact, in the damn world."

This kind of talk troubled me. I was running out of money. I'd been living with Sylvia now for close to a month and had paid her fifty dollars a week for the privilege. I quickly concluded that whether The Cheddar House makes it or not, I had a window of opportunity to learn a skill. I had better pay attention and learn everything I could about bartending because it might be the only way to support myself in the short term. What the long term held for me I hadn't a clue and at this very moment I couldn't see past today. I was getting very paranoid.

If Jason asked me to make an assortment of drinks, I was screwed. It wasn't like I was totally ignorant of how to mix the most popular drinks. Ok, I must admit, I was totally ignorant. I didn't know anything about tending bar and concluded, that at anytime, I would be exposed and let go. I wondered why Jason, hadn't asked for my resume and years of experience as he had the other hires I was told. Then it dawned on me. It was in his stare, that unsettling look on is face, every time his eyes drifted in my direction. I concluded (although I was disappointed in myself that it took me this long) Jason didn't hire me to attend bar, he hired me for, although I was not totally sure, that something, something else.

Panic started to set in. I needed to learn to tend bar as quickly as possible. It was my only hope of landing a job and making enough money to support myself . I wished I had other skills but the truth was I had none. Just a high school education, where truthfully, I hadn't learned a damn thing. Not one thing of value other than what I learned in the back seat of a twenty year old run down blue Chevrolet. And that I could have learned anywhere and in some other places, and not frozen my ass off as the consequence.

I first met Rosie, several days after I was hired. She was everything I was not. She was black and obvious since I was Norwegian, I was whiter than snow. She was older than me by some twenty years, a seasoned pro at tending bar and the complete 'show and tell' of how to survive the city and life in general. As she said and seemed to be damn proud of, she'd been around the block more than a few times. She was attractive in a way (a worn Whitney Huston) that was flattering but standoffish, like an old car with a new coat of paint. It drew one to pay attention but whether a man wanted it as the only car in his garage or Rosie as the only woman on his arm was questionable, Her three previous marriages indicated he did not. Serious but occasionally playful throughout the day, Rosie presented herself as a woman who was deeply scarred but incredibly courageous in facing her demons. As Sylvia came into my life to provide shelter, I felt God (I was getting more religious by the day) put Rosie in my path to provide counsel and yes, yes, yes, a crash course in conjuring up every drink in the bar.

"Rosie, can I confide in you?"

"Well, I'm no damn priest, but yeah kid, whatever you have a compulsion to tell me, I will keep it close to my vest."

"Well, then, Jason hired me as a bartender but honestly...."

"Kid, when you talk to me, I don't want to be put me in a position where I have to determine whether you are telling me the truth here or dropping piece-of-shit lies on me. So let's start out with this one premise, Ok? That whatever you tell me and I tell you is, like in a court of law,, it's nothing but the truth, the damn unfiltered truth.

I extended my hand and Rosie extended me hers . We shook hands.

"Agreed."

I shook my head, yes.

"Then go on."

"We'll I know nothing about tending bar and couldn't mix a drink if I tried."

"No shit. That's quite obvious."

"It is?"

"Yes, it is. Have you ever heard of the expression "a fish out of water?""

"Of course, I have. I'm from Wisconsin."

"Well, that's what you are child. "You're a damn "fish out of water" in a bar. It's just the way you carry yourself . You're really uncomfortable in a restaurant and bar setting. In an environment like this or any damn bar. If you can't command respect then you can't control the action and your clientele, and your livelihood will eventually slip away from you. You have to understand as "a fish out of water" this might not be the best place for you. Because honestly the bar and restaurant business is full of piranhas, and child, you look and act like you can be eaten alive."

"We'll then Rosie, I'm asking you if you will teach me to tend bar. I mean I don't have a lot of money but the little I have, I mean, like bartending is the only option I have at this moment to support myself and I really need a crash course to get me through."

Rosie grabbed my hand, "Look young lady, you damn well are a pretty little thing. And to say bartending is your only option, that is just not true. You're a woman, well more like a girl, and a girl like you has a bunch of options. Me, not so many. But a pretty thing like you can always make a living. You hear what I'm telling you? You might not like the options, but options you have."

"I just need to hold on to this job."

"Well girl if this is the place you want to be, a world of money, sex, infidelity, secrets, thievery, alcohol and drugs, which for the most part defines this world we find ourselves in, then we'd best prepare you for it."

I couldn't believe what Rosie was saying to me. I couldn't be more grateful. God had gifted me again, first Sylvia and now Rosie. I couldn't have been more grateful. Indeed Rosie was my second arch angel.

"And as for the reason Jason hired you, you damn well know his intentions. You're a sweet young thing that he wants to strip to the bone. Jason's a snake. Keep the hell away from him."

Rosie took me under her wing. She was positioned at The Cheddar House to work the night shift, which suited her schedule very well since she was a full time day bartender, across town in a local dive, called Tully's. The plan, was that I would accompany her during the day, and she would teach me everything she knew about making drinks and tending bar, (not everything) because as I imagined, and my father strongly supported, you never tell everything to anybody. Some things should be locked up in your personal vault, deep inside, not to be shared. Only for you to keep, yours alone and nobody else's."

"You won't be serving those highfalutin drinks here at a bar like this. This here "Tullys" is a blue collar bar. It's for the hard working people of the world, not the white-collar high rollers , like at the Financial Center. The folks here are "boilermaker kind of people."

"Boilermaker?"

"Yeah, like a shot of whiskey and a beer chaser. Like maybe a shot of Makers, Mark bourbon and a PBR, Pabst Blue Ribbon beer."

I had a lot to learn, like a lot, and I hoped I had enough time to learn it all, or at least enough to get under the tent and learn as I went, before Jason truly tested me. Test me for what was the question?

Tully's was slow during the day, which was exactly the reason Rosie needed a night job. The slowness wasn't good for her pocketbook, but was great for me because we had the time to really explore the entire bar options. I was all eyes and ears.

It was my first day, and Rosie (bless her), was prepared to show me the way and immediately handed me a piece of paper, laminated, so I couldn't damage it with water or drinks. On one side was written: The Eight Things a Bartender Needs to Know, and on the flip side was, "The Ten Things a Bartender Never Should Do. I read them.

THE EIGHT THINGS A BARTENDER NEEDS TO KNOW

1) **The bar is a stage.** Everyone watches you all the time. You are the center of it, the primary performer. You need to be "on". Show time all the time.

2) **It isn't about you.** It's about the customer: If you don't have people sitting at your bar, you don't have a job. You must cater to everyone in the establishment. Each patron is your guest. Treat them as such.

3) **Serving alcohol must be taken seriously.** Bartending is not a game. It is a serious responsibility. Pay attention to the amount your customers are drinking, what's in their drinks, how quickly they are consumed, if the patrons are eating. *Just pay attention*

4) **The bar is a living thing.** There's always something to do behind it. A clean bar is paramount but never forget, it is supported by a full stock of liquor, precise organization, setting up for the next shift.

5) **Move with purpose:** God gave you two hands. Use them. If you are bartending with one arm, you are not a bartender. God gave you two eyes. Use

them. If you don't know the order in which your patrons sat at the bar, you are working blind.

6) **Count:** You must be able to count the pour, providing consistency to each drink. Each liquor and pour spout has a different personality. Get to know them. Know the price and cash bar, be able to do the math in your head. You don't have the luxury of running back to the computer every time a drink is sold. Most importantly, know the consumption of each patron. You need to know when to stop serving. You need to know when to call a cab, an Uber or Lyft.

7) **Every customer is different**. Find out where the difference lies and provide them the services they need. Businessmen might want a quick lunch and be gone. An elderly man might want to linger and talk the afternoon away. Sport fans might just want to watch the TV screen in public. Girls might just want to flirt and play up to their audience. A good bartender can control it all.

8) **A bartender has license.** Unlike other jobs, you can say and talk about things and subjects those in other professions can't: i.e. dirty jokes, swearing, sex, and anything else that matters. Bartenders are part counselors, priests, brokers, friends, co-conspirators. A bartender is a chameleon and changes to the tune of each customer as they present themselves.

Then I flipped the card over and read the other side.

THE ELEVEN THINGS A BARTENDER SHOULD NEVER DO

1) **The failure of not preparing and or restocking the bar for the next shift.** Repetitive incidents disqualifies a bartender from ever working in a bar and restaurant ever again. The food and beverage industry is a cottage trade industry. It is a culture where news travels fast, and No other bartenders want to work with some one who can't keep a well organized and clean bar.

2) **Drink on the job.** The bartender has an advantage when he/or she is sober but none when drunk. One, two or three drinks, it doesn't matter. There should be no drinking behind the bar.

3) **Be on an electronic device.** Behind the bar is no place to be on a cellphone or electronic device. A bartender's only focus should be on the customer, not Facebook or Twitter, or Snapchat.

4) **Forget to wash your hands.** Cleanliness is next to godliness. You can't have an obsessively clean, sanitized bar without washing your hands frequently.

5) **Fail to have manicured hands and nails.** Your customers will constantly be watching your hands all night. Your hands are the delivery system for all your drinks. They should always be properly cared for.

6) **Fail to dress appropriately.** At the bar, a bartender showcases his/her skills. The attire for the job is as critical as the right costume for the stage. Women who are amply endowed should show decorum. They don't want their male patrons dribbling and tripping over themselves at the bar.

7) **Touch your face or nose.** Beware of the tendency of people (bartenders and otherwise) to frequently touch areas of their body that are off limits and should be limited to while showering. A person touches his/her face seventeen times a hour.

8) **Charge for alcoholic drinks when your customer is drinking none.** Treat your customers fairly and be a credit to your profession. To have a loyal following at your bar means you treat everyone the same, fairly and honestly.

9) **Stay in or concentrate on one area of the bar.** As a bartender, you should have eyes in back of your head. Never standing in place, you should constantly walk the perimeter of the bar looking for ways to service your patrons.

10) **Chat with friends or significant others.** The bar is a place of business and like any other and should not be a clubhouse for family and friends. They are customers and should be treated as such.

11) **Over-serve. Over-serve. Over-serve.** There is a moral tenure to bartending and that is to look out

for the welfare of your customer and **never, never, never over-serve.**

"I read it three times."

"Read it again."

"But I read it three times."

"It's my classroom. It's my rules. We have three more hours here. Sit in that chair in the corner and read it until my shift is over. I want it ingrained in that pretty blonde skull of yours. This is like building a house. We need to firm up the foundation before we build the structure There are three more rules that should and will be added. These are important and critical, if not more so than the rest, because as a bartender, you'll be swimming in these turbulent waters. The first one is commonsense. It's already been mentioned but I see it as my duty to emphasize it again.

"**Never steal from a patron or the house.** Many bartenders feel that their job is a damn license to steal but once caught, their reputation is shit and they'll never get another bartender or service job again, mark my words. and with this social media crap , they'll be all over the Internet and marked as an unemployable. And you'll be limping back to your cheese head place in Wisconsin, wherever the hell that is."

"Viroqua."

"Yeah, wherever and whatever the hell that is."

"Next to Germantown."

"Yeah, yeah, screw it already.

"**The next cardinal rule is keeping a secret**. You're going to be told a lot of shit at the bar by people who would probably tell you nothing when sober. But after a couple of drinks they'll rattle off their whole life story.

They will tell you, especially you, because you look as pure and innocent as the new fallen snow and threaten them not in the least. The next morning a lot of them will wake up and not remember one word they said. Those who do, will shiver in their underwear, thinking they have dropped a f-bomb on themselves and then will return to the bar and test you to see what you know, what you're willing to tell and to what extent you have knowledge."

"Let me tell you this, sugar britches. You need to learn how to keep a secret and take all of them to your grave. The essence is you never know what your patron ism going to say, and sometimes, the majority of times, you don't even know who your patrons are, which could be dangerous to you."

"And the next and very important last cardinal rule, which is incredibly difficult to enforce is:

Have sex with any of the restaurants /and/ or bar's management, wait staff or patrons, because it has nothing to do with reason. Reason here takes a second seat because we're talking about young, attractive people everywhere, and raging hormones and the accessibility of sex because this is what the bar business is all about. It's about illusion, escaping reality, camaraderie, clubmanship, and group think. and especially hooking up. After a few cocktails, it seems that everybody's hormones are in a uproar. The better or probably worse part of people come out and the married guy, out with the boys, having a few drinks will find him/herself doing shit he never thought he ever would."

"Women are the same. Out with their ya - ya, sister-hood. They dance to a different tune once they break from the corral. It's just the way it is. It's just human nature at its best /slash/worse. So no matter what bartender experiences, in his/her diary of stories there will be one or a bunch of how a person's hormones had gotten the best of them. Case in point:

Rosie, then proceeded to tell me about her friend Henrietta who was working one of the bars at Logan Airport.

"My girlfriend Henrietta was working one of the bars at Logan. It was about three p.m. on a Thursday afternoon and this cute thirty-something girl, some-thing like you sugar-britches, was sitting at the bar. Henrietta assumed she was married because she had a diamond on her finger. She was sipping margaritas but her behavior was suspect. Being it was three o'clock in the afternoon, there were a few seats open at the bar. In fact one right next to her, which was quickly occu-pied by this young man who Henrietta thought was in his late twenties or early thirties as well. He looked like a businessman, suit, briefcase and all.

"Wow, I think I know where this is going."

"I wouldn't be surprised if you do, but I'll continue on anyway. He looked like a businessman, suit, brief-case and all. Seeing what she was drinking he ordered a margarita, as well. She quickly drank hers down and ordered another. Within minutes, they were engaged in conversation. The gentlemen ordered another and then another and the woman followed suit. Of course Henrietta was watching with a discerning eye, but it wasn't like these folks were driving or flying a plane, I mean, they were just passengers. So for the pure joy of entertainment, she served up the drinks as ordered. Henrietta said before long both of them slipped off their wedding rings and she overheard, the woman say."

"Shit, I think I missed my flight. Screw it, there'll be another one to Albuquerque. Screw it. Let's have another drink."

"Bet ya, he did"

"Damn right Nora but that was a really easy bet."

"Henrietta,, was now all tied to the drama. She served them two more. They were now falling all over each other. Henrietta walked down to the other end of the bar and as she turned, she found the two patrons gone without paying their tab but their suitcases were left behind. Quickly the two bar stools were taken and Henrietta wheeled their luggage behind the bar. Deciding whether she would call the police or TSA, she would wait a few minutes to see if they returned, which she really hoped they would, being they were definitely over-served and she could see herself in serious trouble serving them as she did.

I could see the whole thing playing out in my head. "Yeah, like I could see how your friend could get herself in deep trouble, maybe even fired and such."

Rosie continues. "Yes, she was now getting very antsy and as she scanned the room, her eyes quickly caught a glimpse of them coming out of the family bath-room across the corridor. Henrietta said she couldn't believe her eyes, those crazy folks went right into the family bathroom at Logan and had sex. It was plain as day. Henrietta was shocked, as they made their way back to the bar, paid their check with a generous tip, grabbed their roller bags, kissed each other on the lips and went their opposite ways. Got it?"

"Got it?"

"Got it?"

'Well there's more to it than this. As a bartender, don't dip your pen into company ink. I mean, have sex with nobody. I mean, no patron, no fellow bartender or server, especially, no manager or owner. If you indeed want to create a lot of discomfort and shit in your life, then don't heed my words. I know damn well I can say this to a thousand new bartenders, but there will only be a few who will ever hear me and understand what I am saying to them. In the most simplest terms, don't defecate where you eat. Got it?"

"Got it".

"OK. now go over there and sit in that chair, like I said and read them rules and study them until you become cross-eyed. It's damn well my classroom and I damn well will make the rules."

Rosie could have been a drill sergeant. She knew exactly what she was doing and wouldn't take no for an answer. She was dogged and unrelenting and took my tutelage as a personal challenge. As I looked at her I could hear her saying, "Damn ass foolish little white girl is going to be the best damn bartender alive. Well, second next to me."

For the next several weeks, it was all about the drinks. It was Rosie' boot camp and she leaned on me every minute to make every drink imaginable, the most complicated concoctions (of course the most time consuming) as well as the basic bar. Although hating to cause stress, Rosie had a means behind her madness.

"There are bartenders, then there are *bartenders*. Any clown can serve up a pint of Guinness and make a

Bloody Mary or a gin and tonic but the really smart bar professionals don't lean only on what they know but keep an eye on the landscape."

"Meaning?"

"Meaning, every bar in Boston has its iconic drink, that which they have created and are famous for. Usually, the average bartender can do the basics and the iconic house brand but that's where the horse is left at the gate. The smart, in demand, bar jockeys not only can do the brands and "private label" but also can do all the iconics."

Rosie steps towards me and hands me a piece of paper.

"Right now this is the list, and every month it changes and it's time again for homework. The best do what is needed and keep up with their customers' demands. The run of the mill let this opportunity fly over their heads like a moth in heat. So "lady drink mistress" get to work, and learn all the have-to-serves': the martinis oody Mary's, margaritas, daiquiris, manhattans, punches, the frillies, as well as the iconics as they stand today.

I honed in on the page like a moth to light, hoping that I could absorb that which I was ordered to do, I couldn't say that I wasn't intimidated. I truly was, Nora Bergman student un-extraordinaire, barely making a C – in high school, never being able to memorize the alphabet let along a list of recipes. I asked myself was I really that stupid or was I just what I at times assumed me to be, just damn lazy.

I confronted the task at hand, memorizing the iconics. Rosie damn well had faith in me. I best not disappoint her. I set upon the task at hand.

1) **The Forth Washington Flip**: Ingredients: 1½ ounces applejack, ¾ ounce Benedictine, ½ ounce maple syrup, 1 egg. Pour liquid ingredients into a cocktail shaker, add the egg, fill with ice and shake very vigorously for at lease ten-seconds. Strain into a chilled cocktail glass, garnish with freshly grated nutmeg drink into a stemmed cocktail glass or the classic martini glass, leaving the ice in the mixing vessel, garnish with a twist of lemon and a twist of orange (from Addie Chin. The *Portobello Star, London*).

2) **Hanky Panky**: Fill a shaker half full of ice. Pour in equal parts gin & vermouth, equal parts, ½ ounces each for a single drink. Stir until chilled and strained into a chilled glass. Garnish with a lemon peel.

3) **Twelve Mile Limit:** This potent Prohibition – era cocktail takes its name from the US law that banned the consumption of alcohol a dozen miles beyond its shores. The very drink it inspired taunts the measure with its especially strong yet beachy combination of rum, whiskey, brandy, grenadine and lemon juice. Ingredients: ½ ounce. silver rum, ½ ounce rye whiskey, ½ ounce brandy, ½ ounce grenadine, ½ ounce. fresh lemon juice, 1 lemon twist, to garnish. Combine rum, whiskey, brandy, ½ ounce grenadine and lemon juice in a cocktail shaker filled with ice, cover and shake for about 15 seconds. Strain into a chilled highball glass and top with a lemon twist.

4) **Ward Eight:** Following the end of Prohibition, Locke-Ober reopened its bar using this recipe. 2 ounces rye whiskey, ½ ounce fresh lemon juice,

½ ounce fresh orange juice, 1 teaspoon grenadine, maraschino cherry (optional). Shake the rye whiskey, lemon juice, orange juice and grenadine with ice. Then strain into a chilled cocktail glass. Garnish with a maraschino cherry (optional). Decorated with a small Massachusetts flag.

I learned them all. It was not easy but with Rosie's support and patience I was learning the iconic or at least some of them. It was to be a constant education because they changed all the time but I was determined to grow as my portfolio expanded.

Nora Bergman, professional Boston bartender: I'll drink to that.

B+

It was graduation day. I asked if she had to grade me, what school grade would I receive. Without hesitation, Rosie answered B+. I was shell shocked.

"B+, you have to be kidding me?"

"If you didn't want to know, you shouldn't have asked. You learned a lot, but girl, you have a damn lot more to learn."

I asked her, how I stood up against all her other students.

"Damn it, if I know. You're my only student. I'm a bartender. I'm no damn teacher."

She and I had been inseparable for almost three weeks, just enough time for me to be prepared for the Burger Palace opening.

The bar opened on a Saturday night to great notoriety as usually happens (I was told) as friends, family, politicians and business people show up to cut the ribbon, and to toast to success even though, yes, even thought, as one of the waitress's said, 'This joint don't have a snowball chance in hell of making it. *"The Cheddar House", an American restaurant in the middle of the Italian section - Come Casa Stupido. Come Casa Stupido and this damn Frank Sinatra music, they play day and night, what the hell is that about? None of this makes any sense at all."*

I was proud of myself. I was tending bar and felt I had a decent handle on it, but honestly most drinks ordered were beer, wine, martinis and manhattans. There were several iconics ordered, 'A Twelve Mile Limit and a Ward Eight, but unlike the several other bartenders, I didn't have to do my research and look the drinks up I knew how to make them. They were ingrained.

Rosie and I were working the 4:00 to 11:00 p.m. shift this night and we weren't very busy which was very disconcerting since the restaurant and bar had been opened for over three months.

"Rosie, what do you think the house brand drink should be?" She looked at me like I had just been expelled from the womb.

"Un imbecile duena de este lugar"

I don't understand Spanish, so I asked her to repeat what she said in English.

"An asshole owns this place" would be a damn good name." Rosie replied.

"I don't get it."

"You haven't been around the block enough, sugar britches. You smell it?"

"Smell what?"

"The smell of decaying flesh and rotten vegetables."

"Don't get it?"

"It's the damn food going bad. Unlike booze, food doesn't have a shelf life. It decays and rots and if what I think is true is true, this place is going sixty-nine"

"Sixty-nine?"

"Yeah, sixty-nine, like the ribs. When we're out of something and its dead on the menu, in the bar and restaurant business, it is referred to as sixty-nine, the dimensions of a grave six feet by nine.

Meaning dead."

"Like you're saying that this place isn't going to make it?"

"Not a chance in that proverbial hell, Nora. It's that catch-22 thing.

"That catch-22 thing?

Rosie gave me a strange lock.

"OK, ok, enough analogies. I forgot I'm dealing with romper room.

You've not been around long enough. This shit is going right over your head. See, everyday a restaurant buys enough food, but hopefully never too much to serve its patrons. Business slows and the food is not consumed. So it goes from fresh to a day old and day old is not the same as fresh. And a discerning clientele can tell. Its texture is different. It's taste and aftertaste and with the availability of good and great restaurants in Boston, people just don't stand for it. There are just too many damn good options. If you're looking for long term employment sweetheart, you best not seek it here."

This kind of talk troubled me. Although I heard it before, I paid little attention. Coming out of Rosie's mouth made it as real as it could be. Damn it, why didn't I start looking for another job weeks ago? The answer was, although I hated to omit it was I was just too lazy. Now, I hadn't a clue what I would do next. My face felt flush, my brow was sweating. I had been living with Sylvia for almost a half a year and was running out of money. I was screwed.

Just as I was about to leave the bar to catch my breath, Jason walked from the kitchen to the bar.

"I need to see you downstairs Nora. Five minutes. No later."

Rosie looked at me. "Don't go Nora . He owns this doomed place and damn well knows its crumbling down around him. Whatever he wants to talk to you about or bring to you. You damn well know its no good. Take my word. Just walk now. There's no damn future here."

I didn't know what to do but I couldn't just walk away. I was still employed, making a lousy fifty bucks a night, but right now I needed every cent. I looked at my watch and had a minute left to get to his office. I turned to Rosie and frowned and off I went in dread anticipation of going to a place I never imagined.

I remember Rosie saying a month before.

"That Jason's a lecher. He's a snake. There's only one reason he hired you. And it's not about your bartending skills. It's about him wanting to get into your underwear. He picked you from the other hens because you're the innocent one. The one he wants to deflower. Stay the hell away from him or you'll be just another bar bitch like the rest of us."

Rosie's words resonated. My stomach was turning. I was getting ill.

To say Jason was uncomfortable was an understatement. He seemed even more so than me. I took the liberty of sitting on the couch, without him offering me a seat. He looked at me and said nothing. His quiet was frightening me. I froze in anticipation that at any minute he would jump from his office chair and pounce on me. It had to be minutes (although it seemed like hours) before he spoke in a quivering voice.

"You know why I asked you down here?"\

"Yeah, damn it, to rape and deflower me." I heard resonating from the wall of my brain.

"No", I said.

"Well, you damn well know, I knew you didn't know how to tend bar. Although I have to tell you, I'm damn well surprised how much you learned in such short amount of time?"

"Yeah, I said to myself. (If you ever knew the truth about me and Rosie). So. that was the reason you think you can screw me, because you didn't hire me as a bartender but rather as your whore", I again said to myself.

Jason got up from his chair. I was damn well scared now. I didn't know how I was going to fend off his attack and damn well knew Rosie was right. I shouldn't have come down here. Jason was a scum ball.

"Because you're young and innocent and didn't have any experience. Even although you lied about it, I decided to give you a chance. Anyway. Because damn it, a person has to start from somewhere. Agreed?"

Jason was starting towards me. I knew where this was going. It isn't like I was an innocent or a virgin. I'd been here before, but it was my choice, and right now, I was choosing not. I was starting to feel a weird sensation. I was getting really angry like something was going to snap in me, like I wanted to charge Jason and rip him to shreds. But then he turned and walked back to his desk.

"I called you down to my office because Nora, I know you above anyone else here needs this job and I wanted to give you a chance, but ..."

"But?"

"But, well, you can see. You have two eyes. The Cheddar is not doing well. We had a terrible two first months and I don't think my partners and I want to throw good money after bad. So by the end of next month, either we improve dramatically or I don't think we'll be in business."

"Yeah, so .... because of that you're going to try to violate me." I armed myself, again for his assault. "So because of this bad circumstance, I'm afraid I have to let you go.. At that moment Jason seemed so fragile and vulnerable. His voice began to quiver. I could see a flash of sweat glazing his forehead. He was in melt-down. I didn't know what to do, slap him or cuddle him. The thought of a weak man made me sick.

Honestly, I wished he would have attacked me instead of crying on my shoulder. It just enraged me. It just enraged me. *It just enraged me.*

Seemingly lost for words, Jason looked down at his desk. I saw this as an opportunity to leave. I got out of my seat and walked towards the door. Jason lifted his gaze from his desk and looked at me through dead eyes. I opened the office door and walking through it, I was about to close it behind me, when I heard Jason's muddled words. I could barely hear Jason saying "Good bye, I really wished it had turned out better. I mean like for the both of us"

Then suddenly, I heard him calling me back. I turned towards him.

"One more thing before you go."

"What Jason? What do you want?"

"Just tell them to shut off that damn Frank Sinatra music, would you?"

Within minutes I was telling Rosie the story.

"Some things remain true."

"Yeah, like what?"

"Like what my mother said: "You can't judge a book by its cover." I volunteered.

"Don't read too much into it. " Rosie responded, "just don't read too much into it."

"Shit Rosie, I won't."

"Remember girl, this is just your beginning not your end."

"One more thing Rosie. Jason had just one request. "And what the pray is?"

"Sixty-nine Sinatra. Sinatra, he be gone."

LEFT BEHIND

The phone rang. I reached for it, and it slipped from my fingers and fell to the ground. I picked it up and looked at the screen. It was Hans. Shit. After seven months, he called me now and I was already late for work. Like a fool, I answered

"Hans!"

"Nora ! "After seven months of no contact, I'm surprised you can recognize it."

"How are you doing?"

If I were honest, I would tell him, like shit, but I wouldn't give him the satisfaction.

"I'm doing fine, Hans. In fact, really great."

"Well, I'm glad and then not too glad to hear that. You seem out of breath."

"Like honestly, you caught me at a bad time. I'm walking fast because I'm late for work ."

"Well, I'll just call you back then."

"No, no, that's o.k.. I can walk and chew gum at the same time."

"I really miss you, Nora. I really do."

"Well, you could have fooled me."

Suddenly, a group of school children, several holding balloons walked by me laughing.

"What's that noise?"

"Oh it's just the interference caused by the wind off the Charles and a group of school kids like on a field trip to Boston."

"I really have to talk to you, Nora. You leaving has caused me a whole lot of thinking over the last seven months. I would really like you to reconsider coming back home."

"We've had this discussion before. It's just not in the cards. I'm trying to build a new life for myself."

"But Nora, I have it all planned out now, our life together. I want you and me to be together for the rest of our lives. We could have a great life as a family. Believe me Nora, there will be nothing but happiness for us. We'll have a couple of kids, and we'll have a complete life together in Viroqua. It's just the right time for you to come back home. Your future is waiting here for you."

"Christ, Hans, are you proposing to me? I mean you're saying things you never said to me before, never in the three years we were together. You wait for me to leave, to tell me all these things. You really piss me off Hans. You really fucking do."

"Nora, yes, you're damn right I'm proposing. Honestly, I miss you terribly. I know it's been several months, but it's better than our regretting we didn't come together for the rest of our lives. Yes, Nora, I love you very much."

I couldn't believe the gall of this loser. If I were in Viroqua, I'd take a Viking sword to his head.

"You make me want to puke Hans. You really make me want to puke."

"What?"

"Hans, go fuck yourself."

I hung up.

THE GOLDEN DRAGON

I remember looking into Rosie's eyes and realizing we may never see each other again, and how thankful I was that I ran into her, as I was that I met Sylvia. Why she helped me I really didn't know other than I must have looked more lost and frightened than I thought. Realizing now, that I was her only student added that much more mystery. I should have asked her why she did what she did; how foolish of me not to have. Nonetheless, it was indeed good fate or fortune. She was a godsend, and although I did not have much God in my life, it felt comforting to have someone or something watching over me, pointing me in the right direction.

In the natural order of things, too much good fortune breeds contempt and here I found myself, not a month later working at a Chinese restaurant in Revere Massachusetts. I was one of two Caucasians, working at the Golden Dragon. The other was my first boyfriend (since Hans) a guy named Marc, who was multi-tasking, filling in when and where needed. I finally realized when looking back, with my long blonde hair and hazel eyes, I was looked upon as a novelty and was hired immediately on the spot. I again lied about my experience which was limited to an America restaurant out of sync in the Italian section of Boston.

After several months I was still living at Sylvia's but I was getting a strange feeling our relationship was changing. Initially, although very gracious and accommodating, Sylvia, never really pried into my business and let me go my way unencumbered. Lately however, for whatever reason she was beginning to question me and was getting a bit too inquisitive for my liking. Something strange was going on and it came to a head one Tuesday night as I was leaving for work.

"You didn't come home last night."

"No I stayed at Marc's."

"Who is this Marc?" "My boyfriend."

"We'll honestly, when you don't come home it bothers me."

"We'll I'm sorry, I guess I could have called."

What the hell was I saying to Sylvia? I didn't need to answer to her. I was just sharing her apartment with her for a few brief months

"Are you having sex with him?"

I couldn't believe what she was asking. It was none of her damn business but for some reason I answered her anyway.

"Yes, I am."

"Like what kind of sex are you having?"

This was just very weird. I was getting really agitated..

"None of your business, Sylvia. Frankly, I find this questioning quite disturbing. I needn't answer to you. I'm not your little girl."

"I just wish our relationship could develop into something closer than what it is. now."

"Meaning?"

"Meaning, you're a young girl, much like the girls down at the YWCA who I look upon as my daughters."

"But Sylvia, they're not your daughters and neither am I."

"Yes, but I was hoping you could pretend to be."

"What are you saying to me Sylvia? There seems to be a hidden message here that I fail to grasp"

"You'll understand someday, Nora, what it is to be an older woman, never married, childless, and wanting so very much to have a relationship of any kind. Hoping someone would come into my life and take the pain away."

I never saw this coming. Sylvia was not who I thought her to be. She was in her mid–fifties and in the strangest way was crying out to me.

"I don't quite understand."

"Big cities are lonely places. Yes, for many they are not, but for people like me, who for some reason fall between the cracks, they are. Do you know what it is to be lonely, Nora? Do you know what it is to come home every night to an empty apartment and cook a meal, never to have anyone to share it?"

I should have been somewhat compassionate for Sylvia's plight, not that I had an inkling of understanding, but for some reason, I was not. I was getting more incensed by the moment. This woman wanted me to fill the hole in her heart and I'd be damned if I'd do it. I had a hole in my heart as well and I knew, it was equal to or if not greater than hers. I feel it each and every day. Maybe it was because my family wasn't around and I didn't have it running interference for me, to lean on when needed. I really didn't know exactly how Sylvia felt but I damn well knew what lonely was. But even with this margin of understanding, Sylvia still pissed me off.

"You might think people can't be lonely in a big city, with all the people ambling about, but in a city like Boston, in some ways, it is almost impossible for a person like me to meet anyone who wants to share her life. Have you looked at yourself in the mirror lately Nora? Of course you have and you see a beauty staring back at you. With your blonde hair and hazel eyes you're a power to be reckoned with. So many men will want you on their arms and in their beds. But before you know it, age will catch up with you and those suitors you thought were yours will be someone else's. A younger, more beautiful woman will take your place. Mark my words."

Fuck you, old woman, I wanted to say. Screw you to a fare-thee well. Don't lay the crap of your sorrowful life on me. I am not your sounding board or sacrificial lamb. I got out of Viroqua and am damn proud of it and now live in Boston. A place full of youth and energy, a place I can feel alive, not a dead end one like Viroqua -There is no way I'll allow you to steal this from me.

"I'm sorry for your life Sylvia but I'm out of here."

Sylvia put her head in her hands giving me just a single moment to escape from her gaze. I immediately went to my room, grabbed my things and packed them as quickly as possible, throwing them into a heap in my roller-bag. I then made my way to the door and entered the main room of the apartment. I expected to see Sylvia but to my surprise, she was gone. I was relieved. I didn't want to deal with her anymore. She was a "Debbie Downer". She sucked the air from the room. There was just no way in hell that thirty some years from now, I would be in a similar place. I made a pact with myself right then and there, at that, very moment, that I would dictate my life. That I would let no person, event or thing steal it from me. That was a major difference between Sylvia and me. She was a victim and was looking for someone to save her. I would never be a victim and never need to be saved. I would watch my life come at me and will control it all the way. I would be the engineer of my train, the pilot of my ship, the master of my universe.

Sylvia really was trying to sandbag me. She really pissed me off, and the more I thought about her and the guilt trip she was laying on me, the angrier I got. It crescendoed I pulled my roller bag through the front door, turned and against my better judgment put the heel of my foot through the hallway's newly plastered wall. I was in rage. Sylvia really pissed me off. Yes, she really did.

YU SUK KUK

Rosie would be grossly disappointed? I was breaking her cardinal rules one after another. Don't have sex with a co-worker. Don't defecate where you eat. Don't stick your pen into company ink. You could call it anything you want to. I would just call it incredible sex with Marc.

Marc was a older by ten years tall, muscled, tatted bad boy. I was drawn to him like a fly to honey. I remembered the first time I had seen him. I couldn't break from my stare and the embarrassment it caused me. Marc quickly honed into my fascination with him. He knew I was interested, beyond interested. I was consumed.

Meeting Marc, I hoped would provide me a few of the things I was seeking in Boston, a steady boyfriend who could give me the key to the city. He provided me neither of these, and our relationship turned out to be one of my greatest nightmares. I was at a disadvantage the minute I saw him, and he damn well knew he was in control. My complete submission to him was one of my decisions that could take me in only one direction and for Marc and me it immediately lead to the bedroom. There was no escaping it. We were the only two non-Asians at the Golden Dragon and that alone brought us together as two outliers trying to fit into a culture either of us quite understood "These Chinese people are really different", I remembered him saying to me.

"Different? You mean other than how they look?"

"Yeah, that kind of difference." You'll get used to it. They live by a different set of rules. I've worked in several Chinese Restaurants, for a total of seven years and they are damn well different than us Americans. They have a different code."

"Like what?", I asked.

"Like its all about "face". It's called *mianzi* It's like respect. Losing it, It's their worst fear. You'll see they go out of their way to be polite, to accommodate others, to maintain a source of dignity no matter what comes their way. They avoid conflict and embarrassment, situations that are uncomfortable."

"Wow, they're definitely unlike Americans."

"We'll their thought process is different. They zig and zag around things. They don't take them straight on, like me and you?"

"Me and you? What do you mean?"

"I mean me and you. We shouldn't try to bullshit ourselves and deny the chemistry we have. Obviously I want to go to bed with you, and I damn well know you want the same with me."

What could I say to him, but yes, yes, yes. I couldn't wait to get close to him, to wrap the better part of myself around his strong limbs, sucking him dry.

"Yes. Yes. Yes."

"Our shift ended at 12:45. a.m. After clean up and all, the manager gave us the keys to lock up. It took us but a mere minute to lock the door and secure the place. Not several minutes later, we were grappling each other's clothes off and preying upon the other like two starving carnivores. I ripped Marc's shirt off and he did likewise to me. We fell against each other as we found ourselves on the restaurant's stained rug. It smelled like sweet and sour pork and as it mixed with the scent of other dishes, like the Gong Bao chicken, it almost made me vomit. But I quickly refocused on the task at hand and gave my attention to nothing but that which was before me.

Marc was sensational. He was experienced way beyond my years. He did things to me I had never fathomed I would let any man do, and I liked them all, every little grain, every little surge of pleasure. I exploded like a volcano. Marc fell back on his heels and finally rested. Exhausted, now lying on his back sweat was pouring from him like a faucet. It was done. We were now one. And I couldn't wait to find our "oneness" again.

Several weeks later, I found myself living in Marc's apartment which allowed me to break from Sylvia, which I eventually did. Marc's apartment, was the same as the previous times I had visited it, but for some reason, this time it totally repulsed me. It was a danger sign, warning me what kind of a man Marc Mandady really was. In truth, he was the kind of man (after Hans) I was now attracted to, untamed, dangerous, out of control, who could take me to places, I longed to go.

The smell of an opium den, as I entered the apartment and the garbage and clutter everywhere, should have been enough to have given him away. It is interesting that I failed to see it during my visits, the several times before. I must admit, I was in total denial, Marc's apartment defined itself as that of a rogue single man on the verge of self destruction. It captured the chaos that was in his head. There should have been a blinking red light screaming at me, to get the hell out of the apartment as quickly as possible and as far away from Marc as I could. It had all the accouterments (big word for a small town girl). His dirty laundry was thrown in bundles in every room. The dishes were piled sky high in the kitchen sink, which was soiled and clogged. There were empty pizza boxes everywhere with leftover crust growing green and moldy. Empty whiskey and beer bottles seemed to be the only constant.

The bathroom was barely usable. There was just a dribble of water coming from the shower head. There was a track of dirt in the tub, and it looked crusted and old. There was total disregard for any kind of system or order. There was no inkling of a feminine touch: no curtains, no pictures on the walls, no pillows, chairs or sofas that welcomed the tired or worn, nothing but the after thought and the cast offs of a undisciplined male. Compared to Marc's apartment, Sylvia's apartment was a palace, close to godliness. The smell and odor of Marc's man cave made me regret for a moment that I had left Sylvia's in such haste. Perhaps it was a mistake, an omen that there might be more unpleasant surprises to come. How could I have over looked such blatantly clear signs?

When Marc introduced me to his apartment, as I looked back to my first visit, he gave me no warning at all. It wasn't like in the haste of the morning there were things out of place or thrown with abandonment. It was nothing like that. For Marc it seemed it was the norm. He lived, or rather survived in the chaos within and for whatever reason it was OK with him. Within a few minutes of walking through the three small rooms, I was shocked I did not hear an utterance from him, not a sound Not one iota of regret, or explanation, or reason that he had so much chaos in his life. And it was now searing me like a firestorm in a wheat field.

"Wow. Holy shit."

"Wow. Holy shit. What?"

"I mean your place here. it seems it was hit by a cyclone."

"What? You don't like it?"

"Like it? I mean like I can't even see it, there's so much shit lying around."

"It's the same as its been the several times you've been here before. It's just stuff."

"Stuff my ass."

"So what are you saying?"

Saying? Saying nothing at the moment but thinking that but a few hours back I had sex with this man and if his personal hygiene was anything like his apartment indicated (which I knew it was) - I might get the scabies, crabs or some other STD. I shuddered at the thought. Again, I put myself in the line of fire. I was now standing in the midst of total disorder knowing damn well what I was looking for (or at least occasionally telling myself) was a little structure and stability (or was I). My past behavior as of late, was telling me that I was not. Indeed, I had to omit to myself that I was a contradiction of sorts, just damn totally confused. Looking for sanity in my life or at least a path towards finding it and there was no damn way in hell I was going to capture it here. *Why didn't I see it before, on my first visit? Why didn't I see it before? Why didn't I? Why didn't I? I just didn't want to.* An hour later Marc and I were having sex again. We cleaned off his bed and got between his sheets and although I must admit they were not welcoming, stained and wrinkled as they were, I succumbed. As unkempt and neglected as his apartment was, I still found Marc insanely attractive and he drew me to him like an addict to drugs, a bee to honey. It was insatiable, and upon its conclusion I just wanted more. As dismaying as it was, there was a sense I was flirting with danger, doing something, in which my parents would be extremely disappointed, something Rosie would strongly scold me for. In light of those considerations, for some reason I couldn't care less, as he beckoned me with his little finger to join him again. It excited me that whatever I offered him he damn well wanted more.

It took me weeks to clean and finally get the apartment in some kind of order. As a low rent housing went, it was now at least livable. I shuddered to think that I was as far away from Viroqua as I was and the comfort and security of my own room (even though I shared it with two sisters) was possibly gone forever. I sometimes regretted leaving Viroqua but that feeling quickly faded with the bustling energy and opportunity Boston presented me, each day a new page, a new delight, insight, disappointment and surprise. I exulted in it while scaring me beyond reason. Marc was a mad man. I didn't see it at first but the more deeply I got involved with him, the more his dysfunction became apparent. There was a reason that at thirty-three years of age, he didn't have a girlfriend and had never been married. Another question beckoned why his apartment had no evidence at all there was ever a female presence other than me. I learned quickly that Marc's MO was never to bring a girl home but rather to leach off them and suck them dry before they ever got to the core of who he was. For some reason, the obvious, was that I had no apartment of my own so he was compelled to break his pattern, and allow me into his life's core.

How foolish could I have been? The evidence was all around me, the empty beer and whiskey bottles, the drug paraphernalia, the disorder, his flirting with the Chinese women at work, his constant drinking and getting high. I should have known that this was a dead end relationship but I refused to see what was so explicitly apparent because I was still caught up in the passion. When I was not screwing Marc, what was playing over and over in my head like on a theatre marquee: ***Innocent, naive, young blood girl, from Viroqua, meets rogue undisciplined, addicted man child from South Boston.*** As I saw it, it would make great cinema but the reality was my relationship with Marc turned into my worst nightmare. He brought me to places I should have never ventured and brought out a part of me I never thought existed. The other me, the flirting with danger me. The throwing the world, "the finger" me.

Marc and I, didn't show up for our shift on a August Tuesday afternoon. The day started with a Bloody Mary late morning (really at 9.00 a.m., when we awakened). After the morning sex, we had two more. We were blitzed before we got out of bed. A drink in the morning was not uncommon for us and truthfully, I found a way, taught by Marc, to manage to drink at work. Another one of Rosie's rules broken within weeks of the first. I weighed how disappointed she would be as I took another sip of the spillover from a Mai Tai. I quickly expelled the thought from my mind.

The morning passed in a haze. Marc and I decided that at 2.00 p.m. we would celebrate the day and our relationship by getting tatted. Marc already had several tattoos. I had none. Whatever possessed me to follow

his lead other than way too many drinks and my infatu-
ation, well, that obviously was enough.

An hour later, we found ourselves in a tattoo pallor
in East Boston. The tatter was Jolly Boy, He was in his
late forties with a Fu Manchu mustache and tattoos all
over his body and face. He was repulsive and scared
the holy crap out of me.

Marc and I were still stoned as we looked over the
hundreds of tattoo designs showcased on the shops
walls. Marc was quick to decide what he wanted. I was
playing defense, clearly not in the zone.

Marc chose Chinese, lettering You Suk Kok, which
Jolly Boy said meant "Give it to me."

"Give it to me?"

"Yeah, fucking right. There's givers and there 's
takers, and its all about me. It's my credo. It's all about
me. Yu suk kok. I'm a taker."

Marc was the most self-absorbed person I had ever
met. I had given him a pass because I thought he was
unaware but he was damn well was aware and thrived
on sucking the life from everyone around him."

"What are you going to get tatted?"

"I didn't have a clue. There were so many to choose
from."

"I got it. I got it. I got it." Marc spits out enthusiasti-
cally.

Marc got off his chair and asked Jolly Boy to follow
him in the small room adjacent to the polar. In a few
minutes, they returned and Marc had a big fat ass grin
on his face. He grabbed my arm and looks at the tatter .

"Here on her forearm. It's damn well perfect ."

"What? I asked him

Marc waved me off.

"No., no. We'll get it tatted and you'll see it when it's done. It'll be a surprise. You'll love it."

I must have been a fool.

It took an hour before the tatter was done . I waited in quiet

anticipation of what would be etched in my skin. It was finally finished. I looked at with glazed eyes. In dark blue letters it said. *Born to Serve.* Damn it. Damn it. Damn it,! I was horrified. I had wanted perhaps a butterfly, or a rose, perhaps a heart or two intersecting at my naval. I wanted something that was feminine, that depicted a celebration of life, not a sign that now I was branded as someone who is enslaved, taken into bondage. I was horrified and beyond pissed off. I had desecrated my body and what Marc did to me was in total disrespect." "Fucking Marc, what the hell have you done to me? I can't believe you put something like that on my arm. It shows that you don't give a damn about me. Now I'm a fucking freak, walking around like I'm some kind of indentured servant."

"That's what you are and will always be, a service rat. It's a woman's place. Men need to be served. That's what you are for."

Shit -twenty miles of bad road. Marc was twenty miles of bad road. I felt used, abused and disrespected. Marc indeed was a use and it was quite apparent I had fallen into his trap. He had me by my proverbial golden locks. I had no place to go, and the price of his hospitality was way too much for me to pay, as the relationship had started to implode after several violent episodes.

The first had its beginning while I was tending bar. Both Marc and I shared the same hours, meaning we were spending the better part of our days together. The relationship became all consuming since whatever issues we had at home were brought to work and vice versa. For me there was no reprieve, no respite to pull myself away from his domineering. He was constantly criticizing everything I did, both at home and behind the bar. Marc's drug and alcohol use became less of a recreation and more of a lifeline. Whatever tips we made between us were quickly absorbed by Marc's (and sorry to say) and my addictive behavior.

It was a busy Wednesday night. Wednesdays and Fridays were our big nights, although historically Thursdays are the biggest drinking night of the week. This didn't hold true at the Golden Dragon. The bar was bustling, and I damn well knew both Marc and I would be working our butts off. We needed the money because we spent every penny we made. Money was now falling in line with the little respect we had for each other. I now saw Marc in a different light than I previously had. He was a loser and it came quickly to my dismay, that being so totally wrapped up in him, I was becoming one as well.

It had been a pretty long day of drugging and drinking for both Marc and me, and at around 9.00 p.m., it was beginning to take its toll. My adrenaline rush was over and I was coming down and felt downright exhausted and full of anxiety. I knew if I felt this way then Marc (doubling my consumption) had to feel more of the same. I looked at him and quickly realized he was imploding on himself. Beads of sweat were breaking from his brow and soaking through his shirt. It looked like he had just run through a sprinkler. The rhythm of working the bar was broken as he quickly stopped in his tracks. He just stood there in a catatonic state and Mr. Ho, the bar manager, quickly took notice that Marc seemed to be nailed to the floor, doing nothing but staring up at the whiskey shelf.

I was working as fast as I could, trying to serve my customers but it just wasn't quick enough. People were standing in line at the bar and although working as quickly as I felt humanly possible, I was also aware that my body just couldn't react to my mind's commands. The whole episode was surrealistic. Everything was in slow motion. I hoped this was a dream, but it was about to become my worst nightmare.

As per Marc's explanation of the Chinese culture, it is all about saving face. This is not limited to certain aspects of Chinese life but everything they do and are involved in. That the bar service was now becoming dysfunctional was a direct reflection on Mr. Ho's inability to manage it. This was a direct affront to him and could cost him dearly in regards to his reputation and future employment. To a westerner, bad bar service was tolerable and a fact of life. Although expecting the best service possible, when there is a break, it usually dissipates when the next drink is served. Not with the Chinese, a service break was unacceptable. It symbolized miscommunication and mismanagement, and indicated that someone in the chain of command had dropped the proverbial ball. This could not be tolerated, since it ultimately represented a total lack of respect for the customer.

Mr. Ho, springing like a leopard, was behind the bar before I knew it. I had him eyeballed but then after I looked down to garnish a drink, he was gone. A quick survey of things and, I again caught a glimpse of him standing directly in front of Marc and screaming in Marc's face. Not Not knowing but a few words of Chinese, I surmised that whatever Mr. Ho was saying was pertaining to Marc's ineptitude and behavior behind the bar. Mr. Ho was now waving his arms and hands, yelling at the top of his lungs, to the amazement of the very packed bar crowd.

I knew Marc wouldn't take this abuse long. He was not that kind of guy. He was wound incredibly tightly and although the majority of his life he kept under control, it was only when everything seemed to be going his way. It wasn't at this particular moment and I knew damn well there would be a point at which Marc would not tolerate any affront and like Chinese fire crackers, would explode.

My thoughts had hardly registered when Marc grabbed a bottle of Grey Goose vodka, from the top shelf of the bar, and in one uninterrupted motion, brought it crashing down upon Mr. Ho's head which opened up like a melon. Blood spattered all over the bar. The patrons were stunned. I was horrified. Within seconds, Marc was on the floor with three waiters holding him down and a waiter and waitress were attending Mr. Ho, who lay unconscious not four feet away. One of the patrons immediately got on his cell phone and dialed 911. It was only minutes, but it seemed like an hour before sounds of sirens closed in on the Golden Dragon.

I was in a state of shock. I couldn't believe what I had just seen. The brutality hit me like a wall of bricks. It was from a person with whom I have been sharing my life, with whom I have lived with for the past several months, who I shared my bed and my most personal thoughts. *How could I have been so dumb? How could I have just not seen? Marc had a demon seed, and by the love of God, it was not taken out on me.*

I often found Marc's behavior a bit disturbing. I overlooked his self-absorption, his constant staring in the mirror or retrieving his reflection from every window he walked past. Marc was also a control freak. One damn well couldn't tell it by the disorder in his life, but with regard to his relationships there was no doubt. He wanted people at his beck and call, immediately responding to his wants and needs. I was one of those fools, who let him wreak havoc on my life. The good news was I didn't love Marc. The best news is that I used him just like he did me. I used him for a place to live, his companionship, his city smarts (although after this episode, I doubted he had any at all). The sex. that early in our relationship was incredibly eye opening for a girl, like me some ten years his junior. The sex. Yes, for the first several months, it was the beginning and the end, one of the reasons I had to break from Viroqua. The sex no small country boy like Hans could ever imagine or would be repulsed by it, if he did. I looked around the bar and it was chaos. There was screaming and yelling and a buzz of disbelief. The confusion was somewhat mitigated when the police arrived. They relieved the waiters from restraining Marc, hand-cuffing him in the process and calmed the confusion by questioning several of the patrons as to what had transpired.

Marc was now on his feet, standing over the body of Mr. Ho, who was being attended to by two paramedics who had just arrived. He turned and looked at me. I was still in disbelief, unable to move, frozen to the floor. It was the most vile and frightening stare I had ever experienced. It was like it was the face of another man, the anger and rage so contorted it, that if you had asked me if it was the face of Marc Mandady, I would have readily denied it. His stare honed in on me, and I could look directly into his eyes, into his soul. What I saw, supported what he had done to Mr. Ho. Marc was a man totally out of control, and his addictions made him even more so. I wondered, with all the liquor and drugs, we had consumed over the last several weeks (Marc significantly more than me), whether he was even conscious of his attack on Mr. Ho. He might have done it as just a response or reaction to what chaos was going on in his brain, probably imagining something that did not exist, with no particular malice to the bar manager. In spite of his motivation, I now concluded, as did all who witnessed the incident, that Marc was a dangerous man and I was putting myself in harm's way every moment I was with him.

I didn't want to speak to the cops. My first inclination was to leave the Golden Dragon as quickly as possible and steal into the night, which is exactly what I did. I was repulsed. I was covered with blood and hoped no one would stop me and question why. I decided I would go to Marc's apartment (thank God, I was holding the key) gather my things and get out of there as quickly as I could. I knew Marc would not be returning, but just the thought of sharing space with him was overwhelming. I had horrifying thoughts, as I imagined the bottle of Grey Goose crashing into my cranium, as it had Mr. Ho's. I was paralyzed with the thought of my brain being mashed up, like Play-Doh and the resulting consequence. I concluded that I was the luckiest girl in the world. I escaped the demented Marc Mandady.

I escaped with my life. I had only been in Boston for a bit more than nine months, and the city was already getting the better of me. I thought about getting on a bus and returning home. It was but a fleeting thought being as I could not face my parents and siblings, and say that my first foray away from home was a failure. I resolved myself to move forward and carve out a life, in a city, that had up to this point offered up only its worst.

I stood on the front steps of Marc's apartment building. It was starting to rain. I was cold and shivering. My roller bag was to my side. I hadn't a clue where I would go. I had never felt so alone and frightened. After fifteen minutes or more, I decided I would foray into the night, and go where it would take me. I had thirty-two dollars in my purse, a lot of crazy stuff running through my head and just a smidgen of courage left in my heart. I took one step out into the rain. The thought of Viroqua, Wisconsin, had never felt warmer. I jumped from the curb. The puddle of water soaked through my shoes. *"Screw Marc Mandady - the bastard that he is.*

It was two hours later, and I was calling on the intercom at Sylvia's apartment. I wondered if she would be awake. It was 11.45 p.m., and after several attempts, I was about to give up on the idea but she answered.

"Yes, Sylvia here." It was time for me to eat humble pie.

"It's me, Nora Bergman."

There was a caustic quiet. It was almost torturous.

"Nora ?"

"Yes."

"And what is it? I haven't heard a word from you for several months. You left so suddenly. in fact, really not on the best of terms." I was shivering and shaking in my boots. The little courage I thought I had to work through this was suddenly gone. What I was now feeling was that I had left the better part of me somewhere in the backwoods of Viroqua, Wisconsin, and might have just been fooling myself thinking that I, Nora Bergman, country bumpkin could possibly make it in Boston or any big city. I was plain country dumb.

'Well, yes and I have come to apologize."

"Really, Nora, at this ungodly hour? Eleven-forty five, now closer to twelve a.m. It's obviously more than an apology, which, by the way, you damn well owe me, but it's apparent you're under duress. That's what's brought you back?"

"Yes I said," in a quivering voice.

"Then, let God strike me down for my stupidity but praise me for my charity of heart. I take it you need a place to stay."

"Yes, Sylvia. Indeed I do."

"Well then I'll buzz you in."

The sound of the buzzer unlocking the exterior door to the apartment building was indeed the best I had heard all day, a day of broken bottles, ambulance, and police sirens, the sound of my spunk being sucked from me.

I grabbed my roller bag and proceeded to Sylvia's second floor apartment. When I arrived, I found the door slightly open. I gently knocked and walked in. Closing the door behind me, I found the only light in the apartment was coming from the kitchen.

"Nora, that you?"

"Yes, it is Sylvia. Yes, it's me."

"Well then, join me in the kitchen. I'm making us some hot tea."

As uncomfortable as I was to confront Sylvia, the idea of hot tea sounded inviting. I was chilled to the bone. I dropped my roller bag and walked the forty or so steps, to join her. Approaching, I could see the dim light shadowing her face. Without makeup (the little Sylvia wore), her skin had the yellow hue of a much older woman. Sylvia was dressed in a nightshirt that fell from her in the most unflattering way, making her look twenty pounds heavier than she was. She was perched on an old woolen stool, like it and she were one in the same, with her long night shirt falling almost to the floor.

Sylvia was startled when she saw me with blood on my clothes. She seemed to jump in place.

"My god, Nora, is that blood on your clothes? Are you o.k?"

Sylvia, no it's OK, really, yes, it's blood but not mine and perhaps I can save the explanation for another day."

"Well, then if you say, you're alright, then I'll take your word for it but my God, I can't say you haven't startled me. Well you must take those cloths off and I'll see if I can get the stains out."

Motivated not to take my blouse and skirt off, I did anyway. I handed them to Sylvia. She put them in the sink and went to her bedroom to fetch a robe, which then returning, handed to me. The heft of the fabric felt pleasing against my skin.

"We'll I can't say that you leaving didn't disappoint me. I know we were sharing an apartment but I imagined more from you than just being a roommate.

"Then, please let me, then ...."

"Explain? You needn't explain, Nora. It was that damn boy . You needn't explain about him. I just know damn well that boy, the one you had sex with is damn well at the crux of the matter."

Sylvia was on a roll. I damn well wasn't going to stop her. I figured she would burn herself out, and if she didn't really want me back into her apartment, she easily could have not let me in. This in itself revealed she had not yet totally closed down on our relationship. Obviously she was not sucking all the air from the balloon, and I was damn well in dire need, and it was obvious she was as well. But what for? What the hell for, I asked myself?

Sylvia and I spent the better part of an hour throwing words at each other. At times, I felt I was speaking to my mother, or worse yet, my priest (if I had one). The conversation was gentle and sprinkled with understanding as we bantered about my reason for leaving and hers for allowing me back. I couldn't bullshit myself, No matter how conjured, my absolute and sole reason for being here again, was that in real terms, I was homeless and a few dollars away from destitute. I would have really liked to think that Sylvia's gentility, kindness of spirit and protective nature attracted me to her but it was none of these. Just stupid, backwards country girl from Wisconsin is sucked in, ground up and spit out by the big city. and is left to fall upon the generosity and kindness of a matronly woman who seems to be in dire need ..... of what?

The conversation ended a little bit after 1.00 a.m. Sylvia graciously offered to let me stay for the night and said over the next few days we would discuss my living arrangements and our relationship going forward. *What relationship?* I asked myself, other than perhaps a couple of weeks so I could get my feet back under me,

Worst case scenario, a couple of months until I could secure another job. I couldn't ever imagine myself returning to the Golden Dragon. And hopefully find an apartment of my own.

I finished my tea which was now cold, reinforcing that this conversation had gone on way too long, then got up from the chair and asked to be excused.

"Sylvia, I really appreciate your kindness. I really am sorry how I treated you before. It really wasn't my intention to leave like I did, after you being so kind to me and all. The truth is I was really screwed up, and believe me, although I might seem to be out of sorts, I'm no more messed up as I was."

"Yes, hopefully that is true, Nora."

"Believe me Sylvia, you can expect a lot more of me this time around."

"Well, I think we have dragged this topic out long enough. I'm sure there's enough leftover for another day."

Sylvia, looks at the old kitchen clock on the wall, oh, my God, look at the time. Well you know you're welcomed to stay. It seemed you might have learned your lesson. I suggest you get out of your wet underwear, take a nice hot shower and get to bed. I have to be at the YWCA at 9.00 a.m. The morning, Is going to come way too soon for the both of us."

I was exhausted, still shivering and was ready to shower and go to bed. I turned from Sylvia and started to walk away. My roller bag following me like a tail, when Sylvia, blurted out.

"Nora, I hope you have learned something here. There's always a price to be paid for our actions. Whatever we have done or will do in life, there are consequences. Sometimes they are so subtle as to be hardly noticed, and other times, they can be dire, totally over whelming, our ability to move on with our lives. The majority of these however, fall somewhere in between and are only addressed after layer upon layer of camouflage are peeled back and we get to the core of the matter and see the strangeness as life unwraps before our very eyes."

Sylvia was beginning to scare me. I hadn't a damn clue what she was talking about and at this hour I just wanted to retreat from the conversation as quickly as possible. I just stood there as if screwed into the floor, unable to move, waiting for her very last word, as to release me from my bondage.

"Just understand that in life, if a dollar is taken, a dollar is owed. it is nothing more complex than that." Sylvia, turned and walked the few steps to the kitchen sink. I immediately retreated to the guest bedroom, stripped, quickly showered and was into bed. The sheets and comforter wrapped around me like a cocoon around a bug. I paused to reflect upon the day and found myself drifting, like a grain of sand sucked from the beach into a welcoming sea.

She had her arm wrapped around me. Whether it was a dream or real I could not discern as I broke from my sleep in a quandary. Fuck. It's fucking real. I couldn't believe what was happening to me. I was paralyzed. The arm engulfed me like a sheet of rain. I thought it was just her arm but it was more than that. Sylvia totally took over my body and I knew not what to do. I had no place to go. I had no idea how to get there. I lay motionless as I had not found, as I had hoped, a safe harbor in the night. Only horror. I closed my eyes and shut myself down and let the night take its leave. I vowed I would never tell anyone what happened that night. Deep down In the recesses of my brain, this experience would be sealed away, as it was the night after and every night following for way too long to remember. It would only be my secret, mine to accompany me in the deep soil of the earth or the ashes of cremation. Whatever it would be. It would be my secret forever, for an eternity that only tickled my imagination, that there possible could be a universe beyond where I found myself today. Not one but many that cannot be counted as they roll into infinitely, and I wallow in my painful little world in so much shame.

SO MUCH, FOR
SLEEPING AROUND

s absurd as it was, I settled into living with Sylvia. Sometimes she would sleep with me, most of the times she would not. Fortunately, her interest in exploring never went beyond the first night. It seemed she set the boundaries, and so as not to scare me away, lived within the dictates.

Nevertheless, I always expected her to breach the security of my bed. I slept with an uneasy anticipation, that at any second, she would roll back the sheets and comforter and her matronly arm would fall over me, locking me into my sleeping position for the night. I was always scared to move, knowing any slight readjustment might stir an excitement in her and she might try to take me to another place I didn't want to go. I often thought of my parents back in Viroqua and how terribly disappointed they would be in me but I needed to do what I had to, to survive. I knew my father would never approve. I hoped my mother might understand but even in my wildest imagination and as flexible as she was with me, I knew she would not.

Each morning, I removed myself from Sylvia's apartment as quickly as I could. I desperately needed a job if I was ever going to extract myself from her control. I was determined to get one, if it meant my applying to every bar in Boston. I knew the limited experience I had, would be overlooked because God had given me an attractiveness that most people wanted to explore and that alone in the restaurant and bar business was a big leg up.

It wasn't too long after being dismissed by a half dozen possible employers, that my mother's words reflected back to me. "Don't ever over-estimate yourself, the world was indeed here before your arrival and certainly will be after". I've heard the same message in another form: "The hardest person to negotiate with, is a person who has an elevated view of their self-importance".

I now fully understood as I looked in the window of the last restaurant that. denied me employment. The manager was kind but didn't mince words. "You're a damn adorable kid, Nora, and that bodes well for you but the Last Hurrah, only hires the most experienced people. This is the Omni Hotel. It only caters to the 'well to do" and this clientele demands only professional service. This is not to say, that in a few years, and with considerably more experience under your belt, you would not be looked upon as a desirable hire but now is way pre-mature and would render a disservice to us all."

I got it. It rendered me desperate as I just couldn't push back and being almost broke, I needed to find employment now. Even my strange relationship with Sylvia might implode, depending on what part was predicated on the weekly rent and on what part on the other.

I concluded that the only hope I had was Rosie. She had saved me once and hopefully might find it in her heart, to do it again. It had been months since I had contacted her but I had remembered putting her cell phone number in one of the secret compartments in my backpack. I sat down on one of the few park benches unoccupied on the commons, and putting my backpack on my lap, started to rummage through it. It took me several minutes but finally I pulled the crumbled piece of yellow paper from the last small compartment of my bag and there it was. My last bastion of hope. If Rosie couldn't help me then I was getting the feeling no one could, and I would have to deal with the few if not the only option left to me, Not being able to cut the mustard in the big city, I might have to return home, that is if I had money to get me there, which I very much doubted being that I was now nearly destitute.

I dialed Rosie's number. Her answering the phone was a gift.

"Rosie, here."

"It's me Nora."

"We'll damn it, sugar britches. Haven't heard from you in a dog's age."

I felt embarrassed, I hadn't reached out. I should have.

"We'll Rosie, it hasn't been the best of times for me."

"By the way you sound, I dare say, there's a desperation in your voice."

"Well, Rosie, I'm sorry to bother you. I'm reaching out because I'm in another crisis."

"Stop there Nora. The good Lord put people on this earth to help one another, so if you need help, and by the sound of your voice you do, by the grace of God, Rosie's here to help you."

"Then could we meet, maybe tomorrow, if you're free?"

"Tomorrow works for me. Early in the afternoon. I'm working the late bar at Porter's. This work for you? We can meet at the Starbuck's a few blocks north. You can Google it? Does that work for you?

"I'll be there Rosie. Like you're the greatest."

"Don't have false expectations kid. I try to do God's work, but I ain't Him."

I couldn't wait to meet up with Rosie and before I knew it I was sitting at a table in Starbucks in quiet anticipation. Then she walked in. I was dumbfounded. I wasn't sure it was she. I was then reassured as she made her way, through the several patrons waiting in line, heading directly towards my table.

"Nora?"

"Rosie?"

"Don't be shocked, it's been four months plus since we crossed paths. A lot of shit can happen in four months."

"Yes, no doubt."

"Well, I'm a lot thinner than I was the last time you saw me. In fact twenty pounds of so. It seems God has a way of thinning those people down who have an uncanny obsession for sweets and such, me being one for sure."

I guess I just stood looking at Rosie, dead-faced.

"I don't know what to say."

"We'll then, say nothing. We're here to talk about you, not me. We'll save me for later."

I tried not to focus on how Rosie looked. She seemed to be fading into herself and I didn't need to pay anymore attention than that which she allowed.

"Yes, about me."

"Yes, you Nora. It was indeed you who called me, and again I heard nothing from you since I last saw you. say three and a half months back, if not more."

I felt ashamed. Indeed, if it wasn't for Rosie's charity giving me her time and expertise, I would not have even survived up to this point. I owed her and felt a deep shame that I had failed to give back, even in the simplest way. One simple phone call out of friendship, rather than duress would have meant so much now, and certainly would have softened the guilt. I felt so overwhelmed.

"Well, Rosie ....." I cast my eyes down to the table.

"Come on sugar britches, look here at me."

I lifted my head and looked her straight in the eyes.

"I'm not doing well Rosie."

"Meaning what, Nora?"

"Meaning, all things considered, even with all you taught me, I just am not doing well. Well, like, in getting a place of my own and a good bartending job. It just hasn't been easy."

"Listen here Nora. Ponder this thought while I go and get us a cup of coffee." It's the adversity of life and how you react to it that defines who you are."

Rosie walked over to the counter, and I found myself staring out the window at the maze of buildings seeming to be going nowhere. It frightened me. I could be lost here. Rosie returned with two latte's, sat down and started over again.

"Did you have a minute to think through what I just said to you?"

I nodded my head that I did."

"O.K. now, the other thing I need you to think about is that in life you have to start from where you are. And it seems the anguish on your face is telling me you nearly have bottomed out."

"Not quite Rosie, but close."

"Then let's use the caffeine in this latte to figure out where we are at and where we need to go. By we, I damn well mean *you*."

Rosie and I talked for hours. The manager of Starbucks kept looking over at us since we were damn well hoarding the table. We weren't about to move, being as our discussion had an elevated importance.

I told Rosie about Marc and my job at the Golden Dragon.

"Did you sleep with him?"

"No, I did not!" I lied to her. I damn well couldn't tell her the truth because if I didn't listen to her advice then, why would I listen to it now? The bottom line, then why the hell was I here?

"I'm glad to hear that. I mean, it's one of my golden rules. This friend of yours Marc, it's o.k. to be friends, but that is where it ends. You damn well know you don't dip your pen in company ink and vice versa."

Wow, Rosie would have been so disappointed if I had told her. Not only that we had slept together, but also that Marc was a mad man, violent, but served up the best sex I ever had. And the reality is I craved for more and the last time I saw him, he was being escorted in hand-cuffs by two Boston metros.

"Well, Nora, its pretty clear to me you need a job to get back on your feet. A job is always the best place to start. Seeing you lost your last one, but you haven't as yet told me why."

No, I hadn't and I damn well wasn't going to. I was questioning myself now. Why had I ever make the decision to call Rosie? Yes, I felt destitute and alone but what possibly could she do? She had done enough and apparently it wasn't enough. I needed a job and unbeknownst to me, that was what she was serving up. Rosie took another sip of her latte and then again, began to speak again."

"Nora, it looks like God is intervening in my life again. I guess He isn't through with me yet. He still has work cut out for me. Perhaps, that has been my saving grace, since my last several months have mirrored your anxiety and despair. So let's talk about me now."

"Yes, Rosie I really feel selfish that the only topic seems to be about me."

"I'm sick."

It didn't take me by surprise. From the moment that she walked into Starbucks, I knew something was wrong. She had lost significant weight, enough to flash warning signs that something wasn't right with her.

'I'm not surprised looking at you ."

"Well, I'm sick and that is all I'm going to say about it, but believe it or not, this meeting was destined because you have a need and I have an obligation to be filled."

I was now at a loss for words. It hit me like a ton of bricks. Rosie, my best and only friend in Boston was sick and my selfishness resonated within me to the extent it was deplorable. Even when she was confiding in me, the only person I was thinking about was myself. *What could Rosie do for me?*

"Nora, as you know, I've been working two jobs over the last several years. Damn well trying to save some money for my retirement but the reality is, as much as I hate to admit it, the more I made, the more I pissed it down a rat hole. Rosie has never been a saver. I'm a spender."

"Well that is neither here or there. I need to make some decisions with what I'm dealing with now and neither I nor my doctors know what it is for sure. I'm just very much unable to continue working the two jobs. I'll retain my day job, well, that is, as long as I can but the one I work at night at Pollards down by the wharf; it's to everybody's best interest that I give it up. You know where I'm going with this?"

"I think so. I mean ..."

"We'll I'm going to quit that job and I think I can get you to replace me. They probably wouldn't mind replacing a middle aged old black woman like me with the likes of you, blonde haired, and big hazel eyed as you are."

I didn't know what to say. I just listened. I didn't know whether Rosie was telling me the truth or reworking her life so that she could cater to my needs. I didn't know and frankly didn't care. I was seeing a different side of myself, one I never thought existed, a side I hated. The thought of who I was turning into repulsed me. I was becoming immune, to those around me. Their lives and hardships meant nothing. What was I becoming? *What was I becoming?* Six months in Boston. Was the city getting the best of me, by every indication, it was?

DUCHESS DARLING

Pollards was a crab shack down by Lewis Wharf. It was a hangout for the lesser blue bloods of the Boston high brows. Those who with their caviar taste and pocketbooks, wanted, for an occasional few days each month, to hang with those less fortunate and obviously less privileged, but who provided hours of people watching and aimless chatter at the bar. It was ironic, that the "suits" as they were known, were really the entertainment for the regulars who looked upon them as the outliers they very much were.

I'd been working at Pollards for three months. As per Rosie's word, she had intervened for me and had gotten me to replace her, no questions asked. I wasn't even called for an interview. Rosie just called me on my cell and said, "Nora, this is your guardian angel. I said you were hand trained by yours truly and that was damn well good enough for them. You're starting Thursday night, the damn busiest drinking night of the week. Be there at five o'clock to learn the bar. Your shift will be seven to twelve-thirty am, closing. Don't be late and damn it, don't forget Rosie's rules. Now don't you dare embarrass me sugar britches. If you need me you know where to find me. You got my cell. Good luck."

I walked into the bar. I wasn't impressed. Outside a small piece of Boston Bay could be discerned through a motif of paned glass windows. Pollards gave the impression not a penny had been spent on it since it was constructed and opened, April, 15th (Tax Day)

1959, as was indicated by a bronze plaque on the wall of the foyer as I entered. The walls were a musty yellow, which indicated they never saw the fine hairs of a paint brush other than the first coat, which hadn't held up well over the years. There was a musty smell in the bar, a combination of cigarettes, food, liquor and a mild hint of B.O. from years of patrons, which was easily picked up by my keen sense of smell. Being a Wisconsin girl, my senses were pure and cut to the chase of what stimulated them, being they were never compromised or contaminated by all the residue of city living although my mind and body weren't as pure as they have been many months before, when I first arrived in Boston, they were still sharp and keen because the purity of the environment In Viroqua had honed them to a razor's edge. In Wisconsin, the air was crisp and clean, and the waters pure and innocent as they demanded one to be drawn by a welcomed breathe, the other to tickle my palate and reenergize my body.

SAD EYES

*H*ow *disgusting* was my first thought. How the hell could I possibly work in this place? Then I thought back not a few months before, thinking the same thing about Marc's apartment. I had never in my wildest dreams ever thought I would lie in filthy sheets, or then again in Sylvia's case, sleep with a middle-aged woman's arms wrapped around me and here I was thinking the same thing, *How could I?" "How could I?"* and it all came down to this one simple dictate: a girl's got to do, what a girl's got to do. I ventured forward, thinking how the odor was going to permeate my clothes and hair and from now on, I would have the smell of a bar rat. Then I remembered, what I had almost forgotten, that Rosie worked here for years and if it was good enough for her, then how could I take issue it wasn't for me? I felt ashamed I was pushing back, knowing damn well that Rosie again had gone out of her way for me, again putting her finger in the dike of my misfortune and calming the waters for me to live another day.

The first person I ran into was Toby Q. He had the most tenure at Pollards and was the designated bar manager. In his late forties I couldn't quite get a handle on his age because he sported a beard, nicely trimmed, black with patches of gray. It compensated for his high forehead receding from its crown. Toby had big blood shot puppy-dog eyes. As a result, I imagined he was a heavy drinker or lacking sleep. These, coupled with the irritants in the air were probably the cause. Soft spoken but direct, he greeted me as would a father his child, a teacher his student.

"Rosie's choice?" Rosie's choice, to replace her, I mean; she chose you."

"Yes, Rosie's my friend."

"Well, Rosie's my friend as well but friend or no friend, working the bar is an art form. It is a skill set. Everybody deems themselves a bartender, like every-one does a singer, poet, anything their imagination can conjure up. But where the rubber meets the road, behind the bar or in life in general, is you can either manage and work the bar or you can't. And the truth be known, it will take me about five minutes on a busy night to figure that out. And this here being it is Thurs-day, will be the acid test. As pretty as you are, if you can tend bar you're a keeper, if not, Rosie or no Rosie you're gone. Got it?"

"Got it!:"

"Then good. Let me introduce you to Duchess. You'll be working with her tonight. Rosie is a great bar-tender. Duchess is almost there but not quite. But she's one damn good, second best. "

Duchess, I surmised, was in her mid thirties. She had dyed blond streaked hair with her dark roots pushing from her scalp. She wasn't pretty by any standard. Her eyes were narrow and birdlike and her nose was a tad too long and hooked at the end, her lips thin and non-descript. Her makeup seemed like it was sand blasted across her face, having no semblance of any design or dimension, other than her makeup brush going wild to cover a few blemishes on her cheeks and a rather apparent bruise to her right eye.

"I overheard the bastard. Second best to Rosie. Screw him."

She stopped, as if to insert a missing thought, then resumed."

"You're a pretty thing. Rosie said you were and by God she was right. We don't see too many natural blondes around here. I mean they're mostly like me, out of a bottle and all."

"We'll yes, I'm from Wisconsin. A lot of German's, Swedes, Norwegians and Finns."

"We'll, Blondie this is Boston. There's the Irish and Italians and a shish kebab of everyone else."

"Yes, I can see that."

"We'll then kid, if you can damn well tend bar then you're a money maker. With them looks and all, just wear them tight bras and show a little cleavage and you'll be laughing all the way to the bank." "I have to ask...."

"We'll Blondie, it's either one of two things. Is my name really Duchess?"

No kid, it isn't. It's Beata Kozlowski. I'm Polish and in my language "Beata" means 'blessed' and Kozlowski means 'goat'." So let's just say that I'm no blessed goat and taking the 'goat" away, there's nothing in my life at all that can be called blessed. Then again, if it's about this shiner here that I'm trying to cover up, let's just say, it's none of your damn business."

Duchess was a great bartender. She knew her bar like the back of her hand and worked it with a rhythm consistent with Rosie's. I started to understand the best and only way to become a great bartender was to work with one. Nothing beats experience and as I theorized, following closely behind Duchess for nearly a six - hour shift, it dawned on me that someday I could be a member of this elite club, but it would take years. That was why Rosie and Duchess were as good as they were, because they had the pedigree and it was built from desire, commitment and time.

Being as good a bartender as she was and a natural when it came to bantering with the customers, Duchess was very closemouthed when it came to her personal life. I never heard her volunteer or solicit anything that could be remotely connected to what and who she was (other than the few words she uttered to me the first night), once she left the bar. In most cases when her shift was over, she would just disappear into the night with barely a good bye.

The other two bartenders, the waiters, and the waitresses kept their distance. It was common knowledge that Duchess had no desire to be absorbed in the social circle at Pollards. She was a stand-alone. One of those who found little if any joy, being around others. I never, ever saw her smile, never mind laugh. Duchess broke one of Rosie's cardinal rules, the first:

The bar is a stage. Everybody watches you all the time. You are the center of it. You need to be on (showtime) all the time the center of it, the primary performer. You need to be on (show time) all the time.

I didn't get it. Duchess could converse with patrons over the bar with pedestrian conversation, nothing of importance or of a serious nature but just hollow bar small talk. But when it came down to communicating with her peers, she was persona non grata. It was like she built an impenetrable moat around herself. If it wasn't for her bartending skills (she damn well could work the bar at twice the speed of any of her peers, me included but I was learning) she would not command any support among the staff.

I couldn't wait to meet up with Rosie, to get the low down on Duchess, hoping but knowing damn well if anyone could break her down, it sure enough would be Rosie. Rosie had this uncanny knack of disarming people, being a combination psychiatrist and mother hen.

Rocky Ruell was the other bartender on the night shift. He and I connected from the very start. I knew by his affectations he had no interest in me and in this I felt I found a safe haven. Rocky, if he wasn't a bartender, could have been or could be a comedian. He was hysterically funny and looked at everyone and everything as a source of humor. My first meeting was critical to our relationship because Rocky, through his dress and affectations commanded attention, but upon our initial introduction, I gave him little if any. Toby Q introduced us.

"Rocky, this is Nora. Nora, Rocky, the same."

We both looked at each other, but while Rocky directed his stare at me, I was distracted from him by a very handsome waiter who brushed me as he walked past.

Rocky reached out his hand, I extended mine and it fell limply into his. I looked at the waiter who was not twenty feet away and he looked at me in return. I was wondering what was on his mind, and hoped it coincided with what was on mine.

Rocky, just stood there and eventually caught on.

"You'd be best to stay away from him." I looked Rocky straight in the eyes

"You talking to me?"

My limp hand fell from his grasp.

"Yes. It is Nora, isn't it?"

"Yes. Nora is my name."

"Well that there waiter, and I know he is damn good looking but if I were you, I would seriously keep my distance. He attracts women like a bee to honey but diss'es them at with the same frequency .."

I listened to Rocky but quickly discarded everything he said. Without a doubt, I was not the same girl I was but a few short months ago, seemingly a life before, in Viroqua. I was different and knew it. I had crossed a line I thought I never would. The former small town girl was now stripped away revealing a more callous and adventurous one, willing to take chances and do things to survive. Whether they were right or wrong, now simply didn't matter, as long as they got me where I needed to go, a place I had absolutely no idea of its ultimate destination. I was now living my life one day at a time, with no regard of the consequence of tomorrow.

Whoever this guy was Rocky was cautioning me about, immediately caught more of my interest. Before coming to Boston, I had a homegrown fear of anyone who had a surly reputation. Now for whatever reason, I was drawn to those who did. This both excited and scared me because although I was attracted, I was not one hundred percent confident I could successfully manage through them. My first several acid tests, with Sylvia and Marc were dismal failures. I was still living with Sylvia and had yet to find a way out, and the thought of Marc coming back into my life terrified me, I still had an emotional connection, I could not cut away.

A boy who attracted girls like a bee to honey but dissed them at the same frequency, interested me beyond reason. Whatever the game, I damn well wanted to play. I couldn't quite break my stare as my eyes watched him parade through the room. Rocky touched me on the shoulder, breaking my trance. "You really will be best off staying away from him"

His name was Trevor. Two days later I was sleeping with him. If Rosie ever knew how I was behaving she would be mortified. It wasn't just that I was breaking her rules but the total 'in your face" way I was imploding them. Sleeping with Trevor was something any red-hot American girl would do because the bottom line was, he was beautiful. I kept asking myself what girl, having the opportunity, would choose not to. My submission was something I was very much able to justify, but sleeping with him, within a couple of days of our initial meeting, was way over the top. It was as if I considered myself a piece of meat and threw myself at Trevor, like he was a ravaged dog (which basically as a sexual predator he was). I tried very hard to justify my behavior, to determine why I didn't heed Rocky's advise, "You really will be best off staying away from him". It was like the more I thought about Rocky's words, the greater my attraction to the mysterious waiter. I was starting to scare myself. Trevor was indeed, so I was told, deep and treacherous waters. A place a country girl like me would readily avoid, as she would back home, read the signs that spelled out the dangers; Dangerous Waters. Do not bathe. Dangerous man. Do not submit. Contaminated waters. Do not drink. Sexual predator. Avoid at all costs. I submitted the moment I saw him. It was only a matter of time and I couldn't be the careful, discerning person I wished I was, but decided I would jump into Trevor's alluring dysfunctional waters with two feet. It was something I needed to do, something I needed to experience from him that made me the low-hanging fruit he easily picked off the vine.

It shouldn't have escaped me, but I was still that naive country girl, who in the big city, was still unable to see the forest from the trees. It wasn't only me who was sleeping with Trevor but the other three waitresses as well. Trevor had his own stable of available girls at his beck and call. I guess I was his Tuesday night special. It was his designated slot for me.

It was really surprising that all of us waitresses in the restaurant spoke about everything else but never mentioned a word about Trevor. We all picked up subtle innuendos, how each stared, how we reacted when we came close to him. The constant way the four of us would pay attention if one were spending too much time in his proximity. Each of us knew Trevor had something going on with the others but like stealth bombers we let it pass in our conversations. It came down to me finally asking myself, *I'm sleeping with Trevor, and as handsome and alluring as he is, why would I think the others were not?* All the girls were attractive and Trevor had a keen eye and played each of us to his favor.

Trevor and I never spoke much at work. In fact both of us went out of our way to avoid each other, which was one damn hard thing to do when you were the bartender serving him his customer's drinks all night. I can't say that for the first month at Pollards I didn't work all night without one eye on the bar and the other searching Trevor out as he darted between the dining room and the service counter, like a rabbit in heat, picking up and delivering drinks in the most hurried fashion. It was well into my third month of work, that I concluded, I would have to separate my personal and professional lives. Bartending at Pollards was a good gig. I was very fortunate to be making a lot of tips, a couple of hundred dollars a night was the norm. I was still living with Sylvia, but now finding a little space between us. Being as I was saving enough money, my desire to get an apartment of my own was becoming a reality and not just imagined. I couldn't get away from Sylvia fast enough. I felt I was pimping myself out for a place to sleep and the contrast I felt sleeping with Sylvia (although not on a regular basis) and in the "love" bed I shared with Trevor was causing me deep anxiety. I was beyond settling into my new job. I was now a regular bartender at Pollards, and had developed my own clientele who knew my hours and planned their days around them. (Or, so I would have liked to have thought.) These regular customers were now the foundation of my existence. I quickly learned who the "tippers" were and those who kept their money close to their vests.

THE PURPLE SUIT

There are tippers, then there are "tippers". It always seemed with the bar crowd that there was one, if not several who stand out and serve up the biggest tips, disproportionate to the cost of the drinks and the service rendered. Jimmy Jingles was one of these. It wasn't the customers real name, James Crawford was. All the bartenders and waitresses referred to him as Jimmy Jingles because he left a trail of money behind him. If his bar tab were fifty dollars, he would leave fifteen dollars as a tip. If his dinner were one-hundred dollars, he would leave thirty dollars. He over-tipped and by his presence, he seemed like he could afford it.

Jimmy was in his mid-forties. He had a receding hairline and a small paper-thin mustache, one that profiled the top of his upper lip. He was small and thin and always wore a purple vested suit. To complement his uniform (women wear costumes, men wear uniforms) he wore a gold pinky rings on the little finger of each hand. Jimmy seemed to be out of sync with the other Pollards's customers. The men were usually attired in jeans, sneakers or work boots, the normal blue collar garb, and the women, who for the most part were casually dressed, some in jeans but most in Spandex. Intermingled in the mix were the outlier business people, men in suits and sport coats, women in skirts and suits.

Nobody knew much about Jimmy. He showed up at his regular time, like a horse to its corral, approximately

100

at 4.45 p.m., for his usual several gin gimlets, and always bought a few dinks for some people at the bar, most he didn't know. Everyday, he seemed to make casual conversation with some stranger, and then for whatever reason, would lay a couple of drinks on them, like it was payment for them listening. I never quite heard all the conversations, but the little I did hear, discerned it was small talk, sports, weather, just regular bullshit "bar speak".

I think Jimmy liked me, not in the biblical sense but rather he always chose my section of the bar if indeed a seat was available. He knew I would give him a healthy pour, which I felt was my appreciation for the tips he had previously left and all futures ones I hoped he would.

MAKING FRIENDS

Jimmy Jingles was one of our better customers and it was a benefit to all he kept patronizing our restaurant. I often thought about Rosie's golden rules and how they applied to Pollard's. Some of them, as yet did not, but there was no question some did. I remember the first time I met Jimmy. He was impossible not to notice. He stood out like a black spot in a sea of white. He wore a dingy maroon suit. It was the only one of that color I had ever seen and it drew attention like light did to a winter moth.

"Who the hell is that?" I asked Dennis.

"Jimmy Jingles" he replied.

"Jimmy who?"

"Jingles."

"Like jingle bells?"

"No, like jingle balls."

"Balls?"

"Like balls, cause ya gott'a have a big pair to wear a suit like that."

"Well he damn well is attracting a lot of attention. The gold rings on his pinkies have to be a pound of nuggets."

"Jimmy is who he is. He's harmless at best. Just treat him good. He's a wanna-be big shot. The more attention he gets from you the bigger the tip. Jimmy's all show. Fortunately for us, he pays to play.

MY NBF

For the first several months I tried to pay a lot of attention to Duchess. In the months that followed, my interest started to wane. I felt I had learned as much from her as possible and being as close mouthed as she was, she didn't cajole me to expand our relationship any further. I fell into the mix of the other bartenders who formed a clique Duchess was not allowed to join. She was indeed the outlier but to my perception, she chose to be.

Although she had as little contact as possible with the other bartenders and wait staff, Duchess was definitely the subject of a lot of conversation. More than a few times, she showed up at work, all banged up and bruised, as if she had fallen, and several times she had swelling to her face and neck. She tried to hide it with make up but the bruises refused to remain dormant and showed clearly under the bar lighting. I speculated, like the others, that Duchess was somehow caught up in an abusive relationship. Whether she was married or not, had a boyfriend or not or children, no one really knew.

It was a slow Tuesday night, Duchess and I were paired up. Historically slow, it offered the staff the opportunity to banter about and get to know one another better. I approached the evening unenthusiastically, understanding that probably just a few words would be exchanged between Duchess and me, making an already unrewarding and boring night that much more so.

When I first saw Duchess that evening, it was clear she had a lot on her mind and was barely able to function. As she struggled arranging the bar, she uncharacteristically placed several newly opened bottles of liquor in the wrong locations. Although she was no social butterfly, no one could take issue with her bartending skills until now. I watched Duchess with a discerning eye. She was imploding into herself. I could see her eyes roll inward, sweat breaking from her brow. Her steps broke in an interrupted cadence as she struggled to maintain her balance. She was in a world of hurt.

As Duchess now strained to reach the top shelf housing the Scotch, she inadvertently knocked over several bottles on the lower one. This amused the four patrons sitting at the bar but drew attention from Peter, the restaurant manager, who quickly made his way to the back of the bar to confront her. He grabbed Duchess by the arm and to her dismay escorted her from the bar to the main office. I settled into my bartending, but wished I was a fly on the wall to hear what was going on in there. Although not one of Duchess's biggest fans, I had to admit I was intrigued by her and would have loved to know what was going on in her life. Not that I thought it was any more interesting than mine, with me coupling up with Marc and Sylvia at the same time.

LITTLE, LITTLE

It was a quick twenty minutes Duchess returned to the bar. There were now several more customers and uncharacteristically, the dining room was beginning to fill up. As slow as it usually was on Tuesdays, I surmised It must be a group of business meetings with the arrival of forty plus unexpected guests. They must have thought like most, that access to a restaurant in Boston on the slowest traffic day of the week, meant no reservation was needed, which it wasn't. This quick occupancy meant a frenzied bar and truthfully, I was happy Duchess had returned. I looked at her and she at me. She had a resemblance of an old yard hound my family used to have in Viroqua. Her name was Little, Little. She was an oversized mutt, weighing in at a hefty 130 pounds and had the saddest eyes I could remember. It wasn't Little Little's girth and poundage that resembled Duchess but rather those eyes, looming as large as silver dollars that just drew me in. Large, bloodshot and wide, they mirrored a troubled soul and reflected a challenging and painful existence concealed within. I really never knew why Little, Little had such sad eyes, being she lived the best life a dog could have imagined, running the fields everyday (or in her case, sauntering) chasing rodents and fowl, and eating into a frenzy each evening then immediately napping out before the bellowing fireplace on the living room rug. In Little Little's case it seemed God had put the wrong eyeballs on the hound but in Duchess's case, I felt the sadness in her eyes perfectly mirrored that in her life, sad and troubling allowing no happy flight of heart, no sustained periods of comfort and security, no relief from what was waiting for her on the other side of the bar when she took her leave for the night. In Duchess's case her sad eyes said it all, and after my initial dismissal of her, I now found myself attracted to her plight. There was indeed something extremely wrong in her life and I wanted to help her bring it to a peaceful resolution, to end the fear and pain, to release the emotional noose I knew was strangling the life from her. I couldn't believe I had turned three hundred sixty degrees from where I was yesterday, looking at Duchess as the fifth, but unwelcome wheel at the bar (since we had five bartenders in all). Duchess was the wheel that just hung on the back of our wagon, that never quite met the road, that if it fell from its placement would never be missed, since it was a used and spent relic, whose best of life had passed and now had only a bleak and worn future looming ahead.

I just couldn't help myself. I needed to know, to break through to what was ailing Duchess. I stumbled over my words.

"Duch .... Duchess. Ya ..... ya ..... want to talk to me?"

She had not expected to hear my voice as she emptied the dishwasher. She looked up at me in a state of quasi - confusion. Her eyes illuminated larger than I had ever seen them before.

"What? You talking to me?"

"Yeah. Yeah, like you're the only Duchess I have ever known (trying to make light of the situation) and probably the only one I'll ever meet, other than Kate Middleton, the Duchess of Cambridge.

"Yeah, funny."

"Yeah, Duchess. Indeed, I am trying to be."

Duchess had a tear in her eye.

"Really Nora. I'm not really in a funny mood."

"Really? Do you know Duchess, that outside of the conversation we had during our first meeting, on my very first day, the words you just spoke to me, seconds ago, are only but a few you've spoken to me over the last four months?"

"So, what's it to you?"

A patron signaled for another drink. I told Duchess I would return, within moments, and I did. She was now standing, and rearranging the glasses.

"Well, what's it to me? I don't know you other than we work together and honestly I would like to know you better."

"Don't waste your time."

"If I thought I was wasting my time, I wouldn't have reached out to you."

"We'll that would have been OK with me."

I was getting nowhere but I was determined to break through to this woman. I spent four months avoiding her and it was now beyond uncomfortable. It was intolerable. I felt it was my mission to crack through her porcelain finish and find out what was at the cusp of the matter. I was now not going to be pushed back. No. If there was one thing Nora Bergman was, it was bulldogged.

I was trailing Duchess around the bar, intermittently serving up drinks, supporting the bar and the wait staff.

"Duchess, really, I think I'm making a damn fool of myself following you around like a rabid dog. So why don't we just cut the bullshit here, and spend a few minutes after our shift, just talking.

"Well, you got to get off my tail. We're walking all over each other and that doesn't serve either of us well. We're making asses of ourselves, and if Peter sees us fumbling over ourselves like this, he's going to get really pissed."

"We'll, the only way to stop it, is for you to agree to meet me for a coffee after work. Just a simple cup of coffee. Just fifteen minutes, a half an hour or so."

I damn well knew I would wear her down. When a Bergman is honed in on something, there is nothing that can stop her.

Our closing shift was like a sailboat without wind. Except for the large business party, and a few stragglers at the bar, we were in the doldrums. The night just dragged on and I would have asked to go home if it wasn't for my promise to meet up with Duchess. Finally, our shift ended. It was eleven forty five p.m. and after cleaning up and setting up the bar for the luncheon shift, Duchess and I made our way to the Dunkin' Donuts on Boylston Street.which closed at twelve thirty a.m.. We made it just in time to order, and upon receiving our coffee (hazelnut decaf for both of us), we walked back to Pollard's parking lot, where Duchess and I sat in my car, taking intermittent sips of the now, rather lukewarm coffee .

"Now you got your fifteen minutes with me. What's this all about?" "It's about you Duchess. Well I mean, not only about you. I mean , about you and me, and the other bartenders and wait staff. I mean, like being really honest, you're like the odd man out at Pollards."

"And what's it to you?"

"It's a lot to me. You're not a part of the team. I mean, it makes it hard for us all. And it must be really hard on you. I mean like, living in your cocoon.

"Cocoon? Like it's my life, and I live it like I want to."

"Yeah, and I damn well know you can do as you please, but you're not a team of one. Like they say, there's no *I* in team.

"Got it. It's like it is, what it is."

"Well it has to change. I mean, like, well like, it goes beyond what I'm saying. Meaning, like, I guess, why stop here? Maybe I shouldn't be, but I'm worried about you."

"Worried about me? You don't even know who I am."

"And that's just the point. I want to know who you are, and what if anything what you're going through. Meaning like, I'm reaching out. Like humanity, reaching out to humanity. It seems like it's the right thing to do."

"Whoa. Really? You really want to get to know me. Honestly, I can't figure out a reason why?

'The simple *why* is that I understand when people are in need, being as I've been there quite a few times myself."

"Really?"

"Really."

Duchess turned her head and looked at me. I took her hand. I could see tears welling up in her eyes. I saw a woman very much in pain. And if there was anyway I could help her, I decided I would. It was a clear destination for me.

"I can help you Duchess, but I can't do anything unless you let me in, and tell me what's happening to you.' "I can't."

"Yes, you can. Whatever it is. It's foolish that you're trying to deal with it alone. Even if there is nothing I can do to help you, I certainly can certainly can lend you an ear. That in itself should help."

"Unfortunately, I wish it would but what I need is a miracle. And or a winning lottery ticket, false papers, a fake passport and a place to hide for the rest of my life."

"It's obvious from what you just said that, you're running away from something or someone."

"The someone is Roydon. The something is my torturous life with him."

Bingo! I got through to her. There was no way I was ever going to be denied. *Bergman's are pig headed. I'm a Bergman. I'm pigheaded.*

"I really don't want to discuss this"

"By the looks of it, we are.'

"But, I don't feel comfortable."

This I didn't quite understand, Duchess, not feeling comfortable talking about something that was ruining her life (or at least I thought it was) hoping there might be a way to break through whatever nightmarish life she was living.

"I have to go."

Duchess frantically looked at her watch. "I really have to go."

"Please stay just a few minutes more."

"For what reason?"

"We're getting somewhere here, Duchess."

"We are? You want to really help me Nora?"

I touched Duchess's arm. "Yes, you know I do."

"Then OK Nora, help me kill the bastard before he kills me."

Duchess's eye's fall to her watch.

"Oh, my God, she blurted out. "It's one, oh, no, its one seventeen a.m. Oh, Roydon's going to go ballistic on me."

There could be nothing more telling than the look on Duchess's face. It was of total fear. One of a terrified dog tormented by its cruel master. In both cases the depth of sorrow and despair were in here eyes, beaten, terrified, no place to go, no place to hide. I had never felt more sympathy for a human being, than what I felt this very second. I was taken by Duchess's plight. I wanted to help her. She looked at me, grabbed her pocketbook and quickly got out of the car. I could barely see her figure as she ran across the asphalt driveway and was gone.

MY APARTMENT
FROM GOD

I t was time, and I couldn't be happier. It wasn't that I wasn't appreciative of Sylvia providing a safe haven, not once but twice, but the relationship that I had with her wasn't something that I couldn't help but be ashamed of. Sleeping with a boyfriend was one thing, but occasionally sharing my bed with a middle-aged woman was another. It was something I had never entertained, but neither was landing in Boston without a clear thought and plan for what to do once I had arrived there. Trevor and I discussed it, but he wasn't too keen on sharing an apartment with me. It wasn't that I wouldn't have jumped at the chance to live with him, but rather that he looked at me being underfoot as a direct affront to the lifestyle he was living. I thought of Trevor as my boyfriend, but unfortunately he looked at me as just another chick in his barnyard

I tried to save at least two hundred dollars a week (which to me was a king's ransom) to support my apartment. I had determined that the only missing building block to my new life was not having an apartment of my own. I relished the thought of a space I could control, not having it disturbed by an abusive boyfriend or a middle-aged spinster looking to find whatever it was that could fill the hole in her heart. I attacked this new obstacle as a driven woman.

Each morning after returning from work, I would add to the stash of tips that I had already saved, and like a hoarder, looking at her pile of imagined funds, what kind of apartment, it could buy me.

I relished the thought of a flat of my own, decorated in young , rag, tag Wisconsin girl décor', meaning that whatever I could scavenge. In my uncertainty, I experienced large mood swings ranging from euphoria to depression, knowing all too well that the smallest studio in Boston would cost fifteen hundred dollars, if not substantially more, Each day I would review the real estate section of the *Boston Globe,* search the web, networking, searching for that proverbial needle in the haystack, that gold nugget that was only visible to my eyes, invisible to those who weren't as desperate as me or discerning. Unfortunately, Boston was full of people like me, anguished and frustrated, unable to find a place to rest their weary heads at the end of the day and to have the security and comfort of familiar walls around them.

I was now panicking, that after months of diligent searching, I had found nothing. I was extremely nervous but as tenacious as a Bergman could be, I forged ahead, but each day I felt I was getting nowhere. I needed to change course. I now realized that I would never find an apartment if I went it alone. I needed a realtor and all the stars in heaven to be lined up. Although, hating to part with a months rent (the realtor's commission) I finally decided to hire a agent and it resulted in the right decision. I went on the web and under Raveis Brokers, I found Bob Harrington. Amongst the dozen of realtors, his name just jumped from the page. Why? I hadn't a clue.

I couldn't contain my excitement. I felt I was now getting closer to an apartment of my own. In my seventh month of searching, three now working with Bob, I felt I was no longer spinning my wheels. My realtor called and said that by luck, a studio apartment, had just became available for rental. These small spaces are usually rented by word of mouth and seldom hit the market. It would not be available for long.

Bob Harrington said "This damn well might be your lucky day. You better meet me there as quickly as you can. This apartment becomes available in a few hours ago, an eternity in a hot real estate market like this An apartment in this price range will be gone by day's end. I'm surprised it even hit the market.

An half hour later, I met Bob at the apartment. The rental was very small but to me it was the most beautiful apartment I had ever seen (cause it was within my financial reach). And I damn well knew I could make it work, being the few possessions I had, could still be packed in the suitcase I brought from home.

"Well, what do you think Nora. This damn well looks like what you've been looking for."

"I know Bob, I'm lucky I even have a chance for it, but honestly, seventeen hundred and fifty dollars a month is a bit too much for me. Any chance for some wiggle room? I mean, like I have a budget of fifteen hundred dollars, but it would break my heart to lose this place. As you know, I've been looking for over seven months."

Bob rolled his eyes. Yes, I understand Nora, the last three have been with me. You do understand that I don't make a damn cent until I rent you something. Like, you and everyone else, can't work for nothing."

Sheepishly, I replied. "Yeah, I know Bob, but I just might need more time to think about it."

"Wow, like Nora, you got to be kidding. You know Boston's one hot market. It's up to you to decide whether you can afford it or not, but if not, but if you pass on this one, It'll be gone in a heartbeat and honestly, I don't know whether there is anything more that I can do for you. This apartment is like a gift from God to you. I have seven more potential renters to call. It'll be gone after my next showing."

I was flustered. I moved several feet away from Bob to give me some space to think. I saw that he was looking at his iPhone. I sensed Bob was running out of patience with me. He lifts his head, walks towards me and speaks.

"Nora, I know you have things to think about, but honestly, I don't have all day. You got to give me either a "yes" or a "no" but I damn well have to get out of here."

I was anguished, I know seventeen hundred dollars is way beyond my budget but also the prospects of finding another studio, as nice and affordable is minimal at best. All of a sudden, I heard my self screaming out, *"I'll take it. "Yes, I'll take it. Yes, yes, I'll take it.*

SYLVIA, AGAIN, AND AGAIN

S uddenly, I felt faint. My legs begin to buckle. This would be the largest financial commitment of my young life and frankly, I was scared shitless. Bob sees my change in demeanor and seems genuinely concerned.

"Nora, are you all right? You look stark white, like all the blood has drained from your face."

I was a bit embarrassed, "Oh, yes, I'm ok. It's just that I'm really excited about getting an apartment of my own and all." I then took several steps towards Bob and extended my hand to shake. He reciprocates.

"I'm glad it worked out for you Nora and that I was of assistance. This is really a smart move for you. You'll now will be in the heart of Boston, where all the action is. Like, you're really an attractive girl. You should be in the epicenter of what's happening in a great city like this.'

I was now getting suspicious. Bob's presence had changed. It seemed his voice dropped an octave and he was sucking in his stomach and puffing out his chest. I'm now beginning to think, Is Bob is hitting on me? My answer was quickly confirmed."

"What do you think? Maybe I can give you a call once you get settled in?"

I hadn't a clue how to handle this. I guess I wasn't as street smart as I thought. Bob was more of my father's age than mine, and there wasn't one thing about him, I found attractive, and I damn well knew he wore a wedding band when we were first introduced. I didn't see a wedding ring now.!

I looked at him and he seemed to be stumbling around, like he was tripping all over himself, and it suddenly dawned on me how I would handle this situation.

"Oh, wow, like I would really like that but my fiancé is moving in with me. We just recently got engaged."

"Oh, then, well, yes," Bob replied, " Let me extend to you my congratulations."

"Well, thank you. That's great Bob. I really appreciate that. I really do!"

Bob doesn't seem to be able to bridge from here. He stumbles over his words.

"Oh, well .... yes .... gee whiz..... Like a pretty girl like you, I should have known you wound have a boyfriend, or should I say, a fiancee'." With a smirk, "You can't blame a guy for trying, nothing ventured, nothing gained."

I am now lightening up.

"Well, if things change, you have my contacts."

I just couldn't believe the gall of this guy. He damn well heard me, damn it. I wanted to say, let it go, damn it, will you, will you?

Bob, finally gets my drift.

"Well, then, congratulations on your new apartment as well. It looks like the month of March is stacking up to be a pretty good one for you."

I responded, "Well, yes. I guess I'm pretty much on a roll.'

"Well then, I will be sending you your papers in the mail. I mean that is, if you don't want to come back to my office and sign them."

I now damn well, would not come within a million miles of Bob Harrison, the asshole that he is.

"No the mail, will be fine."

I reached out and shook Bob's hand again.

"Bob, turns and walks away. I watch him as he walks two blocks and disappears into a maze of buildings. I just couldn't help myself. I found myself jumping in the air and screaming. *"Hurrah! Hurrah! My own apartment. Fucking hurrah!"*

My prayers had been answered (the few I said, shame on me). It was the most beautiful apartment I could have imagined. Six hundred square feet in total. It was a studio, leaving little to my ambitious intent in regards to furnishing it. This turned out to be a positive thing, being at a great address, 5 Fan Pier Blvd. and renting for seventeen hundred, ninety five dollars (way more than I wanted to spend) a month, there wasn't much left over from my monthly income after. I eventually saved enough to purchase a small desk and sofa-bed, hang a few cone curtains but nothing more. I laughed thinking that even if I had the financial means, my decorative skills, would fall to Viroqua country girl chic, which was a visual experience ad nauseam.

Having now signed the papers for my apartment, my puzzle was almost complete, other than my telling Sylvia, I was going to leave for the second time. It was not something I was looking forward to, as I was very uncertain how she would react. As funny as it seemed, I now looked upon her as a mother would her child. We had now reversed roles. Sylvia, had become the innocent who weighed on me. I felt her vulnerability in all our conversations. Her innate desire to want more from our relationship than I was willing to give, as she occasionally cuddled up to me and broke my rem sleep. I knew whatever she was seeking, I was unable to provide. Whatever had caused the "hole in her heart" I hadn't a clue, but I knew I needed to escape from the responsibility of producing anything positive for her. I no longer could be her low-hanging fruit, picked from the tree, when she wished. It was my time. I was long overdue.

As torturous as it seemed, I made my way to Sylvia's apartment. I hoped she wasn't there. The coward in me thought leaving a good-bye note would be appropriate enough, under the circumstance, possibly more than that but then again, I knew my father hadn't sired any cowards, so as I pulled my shoulders back and pushed forth my chest, I decided I needed to confront Sylvia head on. Face to face, Woman to woman. I walked up the two story staircase, focused on the first time I met Sylvia, when I felt so lost and insecure. The reality was that she had provided a respite for me at that very unsettling time in my life, and no matter how I felt at this moment, I did owe her in a big way . When I initially arrived in Boston and then again, the time I returned to her after my episode with Marc, when I had nowhere to go. Sylvia had played a meaningful role in my new life. For that I owed her a debt of gratitude, which was softening my approach, as I was now six feet from her apartment door.

With hesitancy, I reached for my key and inserted it into the lock. The door swung open. It was nearing seven p.m. and I could smell the aroma of something cooking on the stove. It stung my nostrils but left a pleasing residue. It smelled like the garlic chicken dish that was a staple of Sylvia's diet, which she had shared with me several times. It was a weekly preparation and usually served up on either Wednesday or Thursday. This day being Thursday, I knew I was right and I paused knowing in a short few moments, I would be face to face with Sylvia.

As I approached the kitchen, she stood before me as if appearing from nowhere. I was so focused on what I was going to say, that the object of my conversation almost escaped me. It was foolish of me to try to predict how she would react. She was a mystery at best. Her face beamed in anticipation of me being home to share her home cooked meal. Her face fell as she heard that that was not my intent. I didn't know how to tell her, that I was now leaving for the last time, other than straight-out.

"Sylvia, I know this might seem to be a repeat of a previous conversation we had. But as hard as it is for me to say it, and perhaps as difficult as it is for you to hear it again, for the last time, I'm leaving you".

Her face fell. Her lips pursed. Her eyes dropped, barely discernible behind her lids, like they were marbles that had fallen into a bucket of milk. Her face turned flush. Sylvia, didn't say a thing. She just turned and following, I saw her walk towards the stove, turn it off and retire to her bedroom without a word. Prepared for anything but silence, I didn't know how to react, but I took this opportunity to go to my room and remove the few possessions I had there. Walking by Sylvia's room, I heard not a stir. Everything was working to my advantage. There were no theatrics, no drama like before, just the quiet of the apartment which resonated so loudly that there should have been more to this, my leaving, her so badly wanting me to stay. I walked out of the apartment and for whatever reason slammed my fist against the hallway wall, right next to the cracked plaster, the remnant of the last time I did it.

I didn't know why I did it. I just did. For whatever reason, it felt good . So very good. I walked down the hall way and heard a loud bang. I was frozen in place. It was noise from the traffic, the sound of a bus's backfire. It was the noise of the city singing out that my new life was about to begin now. *I felt free. Frightening* so!

JIMMY JANGLES

It was a crazy night at Pollards. Both the bar and the restaurant were packed to capacity. Thank God, it was Friday night, so all the bartenders and wait staff were working.

It must have been a full moon because Jimmy Jingles arrived two hours before his usual time and soon after a lot of regulars started trailing in. It seemed everybody had left work early today. Whether businessperson or blue collar worker, something was drawing them. I was elated, now with the burden of my new apartment, I desperately needed the money.

A busy bar leaves very little time for conversation but a lot of interesting interaction on the other side. Things were really ramping up as more and more drinks were being served. I saw people coupling up all over, customers who but a few hours ago were strangers. A few left together and I ventured a smile as several were most unlikely pairs. Knowing two or three of them were married, I chuckled to think, what kind of Saturday they would wake to (and with whom), knowing they had violated their marriage vows. It always amazed me, how a few drinks gave people license to act outside of who they truly were or show their truest selves which they had spent a life time hiding from their significant others.

The night flew by and before I knew it, it was ten p.m., just two hours to closing. The crowd had really thinned out. It seemed there were other destinations beyond Pollards for many of the patrons, and Pollards was just a place to prime their pump for what lay ahead.

Six hours after arriving, Jimmy Jingles was still sitting at the bar. Since he usually spent several hours at Pollards but seldom any more, he was out of character as he sucked down the last gulp of a watered down gin gimlet. I didn't know how many drinks he had had. The bar was so busy. I had lost track but after six-plus hours later, it signaled probably too many. I hesitated to engage him in conversation, not knowing what would be on the other end of it. I decided there was no way he could be sober, after so many hours spent. I was becoming concerned. Pollard's management was intolerant of one of their patrons being over-served and it would take a heavy toll on the wait staff fingered, resulting in loss of hours during the busiest and lucrative shifts, and possibly dismissal or even worse.

I was really frightened that if Jimmie spoke, he would be incoherent or if he got off his bar stool, he might fall directly on his face. I was suddenly frightened that my indiscretion in not adhering to one of Rosie's golden bar rules, *Never Over-Serve,* could cost me my job.

Boston held tight rein on its restaurants and bars. Not a few were shut down for weeks, months or permanently, because they served a minor or over-served. It took only one time, a patron getting hurt, or hurting others, driving intoxicated or the worst of all fears, getting into an accident and causing bodily harm, even death, that lives would be ruined forever. In circumstances such as this everyone would be liable, the restaurant, bar, bartender, patron, any and all who were connected to the event. There would be no safe haven, just endless litigation, with very little hope of recovering. I shuddered at the thought.

While the other bartenders were catering to their patrons, I honed in on Jimmie. I needed to gauge his temperature, to see if I was correct or (hopefully) wrong and if he still was coherent and had all his faculties. I approached him and leaned over the bar to get a better assessment. He leaned forward to meet me half way.

"Jimmie, you O.K?"

"O.K., meaning .... ?" he asked in a garbled tone.

"O.K., meaning again, have you had too much to drink?"

"Meaning again"

I was starting to get really pissed pissed off.. There was too much at stake to play at this. My job. My beautiful apartment. I figured I would take another approach.

"Jimmy you need to help me."

"Help you, meaning what?"

I was losing it. Patience isn't my best trait. I grabbed Jimmy by the shoulder.

"Jimmie, you've been sitting at this bar for some six hours. Some people are concerned you've had too much to drink. Me, being one."

"So?"

"So, if that is indeed true than you have an hour or so to sober up and there's just no way in hell, that you're getting in a car to drive."

"No, need to worry. Jimmy lives in town."

I was instantly relieved, at least that was part of the equation I needn't worry about but Jimmie, without a doubt was intoxicated.

"You worried about me?"

"Yes, I damn well am concerned and I hope you drink some coffee and stay at the bar until closing. Honestly, Jimmy, this is unlike you, you're usually here by five and gone by seven. Today you were in at three-thirty and haven't left yet. You celebrating or something?"

"Nora!"

"Yes",

I was getting very frustrated now. Jimmy was slurring his words. He was almost unintelligible but he held my attention, as he stared intensely at me absorbing all the energy in the room.

I was leaning over the bar as far as I could, standing on the tips of my toes. I could feel them digging into the front of my Reebok sneakers, the most comfortable shoes I had, which I usually wore tending bar. Jimmy elevated himself off his seat and as I scanned the bar. No one was paying attention.

"Nora, Nora!"

"Christ, Jimmy, I damn well can hear you."

"You can't tell anyone, but I'm in serious trouble."

"Jimmie, what do you mean serious trouble?"

"I mean *serious trouble.*"

Jimmy Jingles was a regular at the bar. We had known each other for months and had a tad more than a cordial bartender/patron relationship. I was getting to know him a little better but always felt he had drawn a line in regards to what he wanted to reveal about himself which was very strange to me being that his dress brought a lot of attention. He was definitely an outlier at the bar and a lot of the other patrons looked at him as a source of entertainment, someone, who was a constant presence who could capture their attention and conversation for a minute or two. I recalled hearing several.

"Who's the asshole in the purple suit?"

"Beats me, but he's a bar anchor."

"A bar anchor?"

"Yeah, every time I come in here, he was sitting at the bar. Usually in the same seat at end. He like anchors the bar."

"Got it."

"Yeah, I heard some guy saying he was hooked up to the Italians in the North End. That he was in the "know", that he hangs around with some very bad people and you should keep your distance from him."

I remember over hearing this conversation and chuckling inside. Jimmie Jingles a member of the Mafia, I just couldn't fathom it. *Sure,* I said to myself, "There was no doubt he had a lot of money. He was always buying drinks for people he really didn't know, which seemed very peculiar to me. It seemed Jimmy didn't have any friends because he kept to himself and totally disengaged from the other regulars at the bar. The only people he reached out to were usually tourists or first time visitors. People he would only see once, or that he thought he would never see again. It seemed, for whatever reason, Jimmy, needed to act big in front of them, providing him the opportunity to look big in front of everyone.

recalled another conversation, again Jimmy being at its heart.

"The guy in the purple suit, he's a Wall Street millionaire."

"Really, ... ?"

"Yeah, really. Made his money betting on Bain Capital stuff."

"Yeah. Story has it, anything Romney and Bain were connected to he bought in."

"That stuff was closed. Couldn't happen."

"Not when it was closed, but when it went public. Like Tom Stemberg's Staples."

"Really. Doesn't look like a Wall Streeter to me."

"When you have his kind of money , you can look like and be anyone you want ..."

"Even if you wear the same suit everyday?" en "Yup, even if you wear the same suit. Yeah, but he's probably like that writer Tom Wolfe. You know, *The Bonfire of the Vanities*" author, who wears, the same white suit every day?"

"Nope, I don't know him."

"Well, that doesn't matter. The point is the guy has a closet full of the same white suits. I bet you "Maroon Suit" has a closet full of them too. It wasn't incongruous to me that Jimmy stirred so much attention. Obviously his clothing and demeanor did not fade into the background as most of the patrons did. His conversations did not blend into the usual bar room chatter because Jimmie wasn't verbose, at least to any familiar face. Again his interaction was limited to people he didn't know. People who didn't know him and frankly didn't care.

I was bending so far over the bar that my back ached. I could smell Jimmie's rancid breath, lightly disguised by the gallon of gin gimlets he had poured down his throat over the course of six-plus hours. I was too close to him. I had to back away. My moat of privacy was breached. I didn't like it.

"I'm in serious trouble."

I can't help you if you don't tell me why. Not that I thought I could help Jimmie, but he sparked my curiosity and I was all ears?"

"I took money from the.... the Gallios brothers."

I hadn't the faintest idea what Jimmy was talking about. I hadn't a clue as to what he did for a living, (presuming he did anything) and as far as the Gallios brothers were concerned, I had never heard of them.

"I don't know what you're talking about.

"The Gallios brothers, they're big. Every one knows who the Gallios brothers are."

I didn't know who they were. I guess I wasn't anyone, at least by Jimmy's standards."

"Is there anything I can do?"

"No, I'm a dead man."

A dead man. Obviously Jimmy was really drunk or he wouldn't be talking trash. In fact he wouldn't be talking (only to impress) which was his usual *modus operandi*. (a big city phrase I learned from Rosie).

"No, you can't help me, unless you have lots of money."

"Lots of money? What was Jimmie talking about, I barely had enough money to pay my rent . *"What's this about money?"* I asked myself. I was seeing if he needed something to get him sober or for me to maybe call for a cab but money. Not a clue. Don't have any. *Haven't a clue what he's talking about.*

I backed away from the bar and removed myself from earshot of Jimmie. He pulled himself back and braced himself against the back of his barstool. I walked down the end of the bar and out of the corner of my eye, I saw Johnnie remove himself from his seat. Gingerly walking, he made his way past the few remaining patrons at the bar, and then to the front door. I walked from behind the bar to catch up with him. By the time I got to the front door, Jimmy had made his way to one of the adjoining buildings, jutting out from the walkway. I just missed him rounding the corner. Into the darkness of the night Jimmy Jingles was gone. I made my way back to the bar.

"Jimmy Jingles, looks like he had too many, Not a good situation for us." Dennis, the bar manager surmised.

"Yeah, sorry about that Dennis, his count got away from me.

"And damn lucky for us, he wasn't driving."

"Like, I said, Dennis .... like I'm really sorry."

"By the looks of him, he shouldn't be walking."

"Yap, I get it. I'll be more careful the next time."

"You better, I have a short fuse when it comes to over serving our customers. You're on notice Norma. I'll be watching you." I responded like I didn't hear him.

"Hey Dennis, you know who the Gallios are?"

"Yeah, they're them brothers. They hang out a couple miles from here."

"Yeah, Jimmy says they're really big."

'Not as much as they are really bad.

BOSTON IN MOTION

I loved my new apartment. It was just what I needed to get my life back on the right track. My parents would be horrified if they knew what I was paying for it. Seventeen hundred and ninety-five dollars a month could purchase a mansion in Viroqua, (that is, if there were any), but so little in Boston.

In spite of the payment, the apartment put me right in the heart of the city. Boston was constantly in motion. There was activity all the time and the city itself was always celebrating something. I looked at the city register and found it celebrated Martin Luther King's Birthday, President's Day, Evacuation Day, Patriot's Day, Memorial Day, Labor Day, Columbus Day, Veteran's Day, and of course Halloween, Thanksgiving, Christmas and New Year's Eve, which Boston calls, 'The Festival of Lights".

When you live in the city, you have to get into the flow of things. The energy itself will engulf you and either you have to engage it or it will work against you. With the constant flow of activity, Boston is always noisy. There is traffic everywhere and the constant noise of car horns is heard throughout the day, with drivers losing their patience as they try to negotiate the very narrow roads, that not a century ago were tracked by horses and sleds. Boston is also the medical capital of the world. There is no lack of great doctors and hospitals but with this again comes the backdrop of ambulance sirens as patients are constantly brought to Mass

General or Brigham and Woman's or the many other emergency facilities.

Boston is also a beehive of youthful energy. There are at least fifty colleges and universities within it and its surrounding communities. Harvard, Tufts, MIT, Simmons, Boston College, Northeastern, Holy Cross, and Boston University, just to name a few. These are amongst some of the most prestigious colleges and universities in the world. These attract a melting pot of talented youth coming from every corner of the globe and, if, profoundly talented, and financially resourceful, they find their way to these coveted institutions, with many never leaving the city after they graduate.

Boston being such a desirable place to live, (although, financially taxing) holds them like flypaper holds a moth.

Having so many talented people and opportunities in education, medicine, technology, and research, and a great entrepreneurial spirit birthing start-up, after start-up, many bright youth, see the city as the place they can find their golden goose. The competition for jobs is horrific, the opportunities however are limitless, if one has the pedigree and all the stars are lined up so everything falls into place.

Boston, being as concentrated as it is, there are stories abound about the successes and failures of those it had captured because as in all big cities and life in general, there are a lot of winners but an equal number of those who have lost their way, as they found Boston very difficult to negotiate and after time almost given up on it. I was almost one of these

A high school education doesn't get you very far in Boston, so in retrospect, I thought I was doing rather well. I initially expected much more progress than I had enjoyed but I was all right where I was. Not being in Viroqua, Wisconsin, made my life considerably more tolerable, well up to this point. I gauged this measure on finally getting an apartment of my own. Small and restricted as it was, it was mine and I snatched it right under the noses of all those who I damn well knew were a hell of a lot smarter than me, those blue blood pedigrees, or those "smarter" than the average bear (me, not being amongst them) privileged. Yes, I saw this as a significant win for me and knew from this moment on I could make my way in the big city. I was damn proud of myself and I knew my parents would be too if they knew of my great success, although they would be totally ashamed of my break away from the Viroqua values I had chosen to have left behind.

PARTYING WITH
ROSIE?

I found myself in a celebratory mood. Having joy in one's life was one thing but sharing it with someone gave it a whole other dimension. My enthusiasm was running away with me as I thought who I could celebrate with on this Wednesday night. I hadn't had a Wednesday off since I began working at Pollards, and looked forward to it, being Wednesday was a damn good carousing night as I had learned tending bar over the past several months. It wasn't like Thursday, which is the biggest drinking night of the week but a damn sight better than Tuesday, which was considered the worst.

I considered Trevor for a brief moment then quickly realized he was so much into himself he would see my huge success as no accomplishment at all. Anyway, I had to plan ahead to be with him. He saw himself very much in demand and scheduled his life weeks in advance, with absolutely no time to have an impromptu moment with me or anyone else. He didn't need to fill in the cracks of his life because there weren't any. Trevor sucked up all the air in the room. And knowing this, I, like, all his other foolish girls just sheepishly fell in line. I was penciled in his calendar. And would again be with him next Thursday after work, as our bi-monthly indulgence continued. *Foolish girl. Damn, foolish girl!*

In sifting through my list of friends, I concluded, I had only one. Sylvia and Duchess, certainly couldn't be amongst them and other than those two, only one person stood out. It was Rosie. There was no doubt in my mind she was my only friend and if there was anything I was neglectful about , it was aligning myself with people with whom I could emotionally connect. *I just didn't try and most times, I didn't care ... but it seemed that I damn well cared now.*

How foolish was I to think anyone else had gifted me what Rosie had. Yes, Sylvia, for a short time, had provided me with a place to live but there was a price to pay. How naive of me to think I was not going to pay the tariff at the door. It was Rosie, and no one else. She gave of herself, asking nothing in return, other than me being an attentive student and following through on her teachings. (How terribly disappointed she would be if she ever knew how I fell short of her expectations. I couldn't disappoint Rosie. I couldn't embarrass myself. So I decided I would never tell her). I reached for my cell phone which I, like everyone else used theirs, used mine to anchor me to my narcissistic world. Her number stared at me reinforcing my neglect in not calling her over the last several months. I could make up every reason I did not, but the truth was my life was a whirlwind and the sanity that Rosie had provided me, was diametrically opposed to how I was living my life now. I had forgotten Rosie's rules. Those, she painstakingly tried to engrain in me. I had abandoned them, as I had so thoughtlessly relinquished my virginity under the bleachers of the Viroqua Blackhawks football field at the age of fourteen. I was determined that someday I would tell Rosie the truth. This was not the time. Finding an apartment was good news and I knew that like all the other bad in my life, I had the ability to hide my indiscretions, to lock them in the gym locker of my mine and venture forth undeterred. So I betrayed Rosie's teachings and betrayed her trust. I damn well did. So what? I could move on from here. Nora Bergman has a job and has kept it for the last couple of months. Nora Bergman, now has her own apartment. These are things that I at least should be semi-proud of. I'm damn well, a hell of a lot further along than I ever thought I would be that first night landing in Boston. Hallelujah. Hallelujah.

"Yes, Rosie here. Who's this?"

"It's Nora. I can't believe you don't have me plugged into your phone."

"Nora. My God, I can't believe you are calling me. I kind of crossed you off my Christmas card list, and this thing about not having your number in my phone, I'm an old lady, and there's a lot of things about my phone, I don't understand. Like putting in numbers and such."

"We'll then, maybe I can somewhat repay you for what you taught me about tending bar by sharing the little knowledge I have of these phones but that's not the nature of my call."

"The nature of your call. Wow. Well, I must say 'the nature of your call, Yeah, like that, well then, pray tell, what is the nature of your call'?"

"Well Rosie, things have gone really good for me as of late, and the reality is if it wasn't for you, I doubt, I'd be saying that. In fact, I very much doubt I would still be here in Boston. Probably I would have put my tail between my legs and scurried back to Viroqua."

"Well in spite of your untimeliness, I am damn well pleased you called me." "Untimeliness?"

"We'll you certainly seem to be full of piss and vinegar and honestly, I wish you could share some of that with me because lately I am lacking."

135

"Then Rosie, I am quite pleased I made the call because it is my intent we get together. As they say, "a lot of water has passed over the dam.""

"Yes, more than you probably would know. Some not fit for bathing or drinking. We'll anyway, how are you doing?"

"Like I said, I'm doing very well and I would like to get together with you. Maybe lunch at Faneuil Hall or the Back Bay. Maybe at the sushi place on James Street. I was just introduced to sushi and surprisingly, immediately acquired a taste for it."

Well, you may have but I'm no sushi fan. In fact, it turns my stomach. There's worms in it, you know. And to be honest I really don't have any desire to go out. Other than work , which I've dramatically pared back. I've become somewhat of a recluse."

"Well, then you better break through it because your girl here, Nora, wants to celebrate with her girl Rosie. Yes you Rosie, are the only person I want to celebrate with. So I'll not take "no" for an answer. Come on Rosie, come on, I just won't take no for an answer. Please.? Pretty please?"

Pretty please! OK. OK. How about Ned Devine's in Faneuil Hall? It's a good old American pub, serving good old American hamburgers and beer None of that fancy, bull crap stuff for Rosie."

"Tomorrow's, my day off. Could you make it around twelve -thirty?"

"I don't get up till 1.00 p.m. O.k. O.k. I'm just kidding. Yeah, sure, why not ? Twelve-thirty at Ned Devine's in Faneuil Hall. Got it." I almost didn't recognize her. I had to look twice before I concluded that the woman, barely resembling Rosie, but at least twenty pounds lighter than the last time I saw her, was indeed her. She was also using a cane, so I quickly surmised that the woman approaching me was some many years older than I knew Rosie to be.

Initially, I thought she was another woman who was going to meet someone at the table behind where I was sitting, but as she approached, I started to hone in on the woman's features and concluded, that it was indeed Rosie. Not the woman with whom I was familiar with but rather a new rendition, significantly thinner, face more shallow and worn, but Rosie nonetheless.

"Surprised?" Rosie stood before me. I looked up at her. Yes, I was surprised, very much so. Surprised. Yes, surprised as hell. Rosie sat down.

"Not what, or who, you were expecting?"

I got out of my chair and put my arms around Rosie. I could feel my fingers sink through her thick clothing. I could feel her ribs protruding, and her body shivering from the deep February chill. He gauntness took me by surprise and it shocked me as she pulled from my grip and removed her coat. Rosie was barely a shadow of her former self. I needn't look too deeply. All the signs were there, that her body had been stressed and was not doing well. I decided I would let our lunch play out naturally. Whatever was going on with Rosie she would tell me, or she would not, but I decided I wouldn't mention it unless she did. It didn't take long. Rosie pulled out a chair at the table, placed her coat, hat, gloves, scarf and pocketbook on it, and then sat on the last unoccupied chair, immediately to her far left, since we were sitting at a table for four and then she spoke."

"I'm sick."

"Sick?"

"Don't play ignorant with me, Nora. there's nothing that upsets me more than someone being coy with me . Christ, look at me, I'm just a shadow of my former self. I can't even find clothes in my closet that fit me anymore. They all fall off like I was wearing a canopy. I haven't been this size since I was fourteen years old. And I don't mind telling you that I would love to be that age again." Rosie paused, her head looked down at her place setting on the table. She picked up a fork and started to inspect it, after which she picked up her napkin and started polishing all her silverware.

"Dirty?" I asked. "Yeah, dirty. Oh, oh, don't mind me Nora, I'm just really quite cautious now about germs and such. In fact, about what I eat, the air I inhale, everything. All the previous mentioned and a lot more. I just don't think I have the immune system I used to. In fact I know I don't. Well, that is since my disease."

"Your disease?"

"Yes, Nora, I have a strange blood disorder that is sucking the life from me. Christ, look at me. I'm just a shadow of my former self. It's one of these rare diseases that yet have no immediate cure. They call it pernicious anemia. It is basically is the inability to process Vitamin B-12, which is instrumental in the development of red blood cells. It was diagnosed, when after months, not feeling like myself, I went to my doctor to talk to her about my loss of weigh, constant fatigue, the yellowing of my skin, my unsteadiness. As you can now see, I now use a cane and such. It took months and a myriad of tests but all of them came back conclusive. I have this disease. Where and how I acquired it, I haven't a clue.

I was devastated. It had been my intention to celebrate with my best and only friend but now I was hearing her fortunes were just the opposite of mine. The air went out of my balloon as I quietly sank into my chair. The thought of what Rosie was going through was daunting. I could not understand how a person like her, as outgoing as she was in heart and spirit, could be victimized by such an intrusion into her flesh, her heart and her soul. It was a clear injustice. I hated that it was happening to her. I also felt selfishly, it was a clear affront to me. Rosie was not only just my best friend (although I hadn't seen much of her as of late), that just knowing she lived in the same city, within earshot and just a cab ride or a brisk walk away made a lot of the things that were wrong in my life, at least tolerable. She was my port in a storm. My respite as life in the big city tried to roll over me.

Both Rosie and I ate small portions. Rosie ordered the American cheese burger she had mentioned on the phone earlier, but barely took two bites. I ordered a chicken Caesar salad but it tasted like rubber. Obviously not from the best of chicken parts.

It seemed that after the first hour Rosie and I had an unspoken agreement that for the remainder of the lunch, we would keep the conversation positive and light. We bantered about, knowing the weight of our previous conversation hung over us like a lead shroud. We were courteous and polite, but antsy as hell to get away from each other. All and all the luncheon was a short exercise in civility, when I was hoping for a wondrous celebration of the few wins I had just experienced with someone who I truly felt cared about me. I knew in my heart of hearts Rosie did, and I damn well knew I cared about her too. But I just wanted to laugh today, but at this time, there was no laughter to be found.

I helped Rosie get up from her chair. She put on her coat and hat, wrapped her scarf around her and put on her gloves, then reached for her cane. I dressed as well and was about to walk her to the door, when she paused and reached into her pocket and pulled out a piece of paper. She turned and handed it to me. Smiling she said. "Nora, just another one of Rosie's' lists. You know I live by them. Others I shared with you but I don't believe I gave you this one. It never seemed to be the appropriate time. But then again, there's no time like the present. One thing though, please do me a favor, read it in an hour or so, after I'm gone, and this one always keep with you. It's Rosie's condensed rules for life. Just add alcohol when needed."

I walked Rosie to get a cab. We flagged one down. She got in, blew me a kiss and then was gone. I knew as the cab distanced itself from me and seeing her look back, I would never see her again. An hour later I reached into my pocket and unfolded the note. It was printed in bold type.

Rosie's Notes To Nora

1) **The world is uncertain at best.**
2) **No one knows what they are doing. We are all pretending.**
3) **Don't spend time with people who don't treat you well..**
4) **Treat those you love with LOVE.**
5) **Learn to LOVE, RESPECT and FORGIVE yourself**
6) **It's later than you think**

XXOXXOOO
Rosie

MARC MADNESS

Everything has changed My friend Rosie was seriously ill. There was no denying it. Even thought I tried to reason through it, thinking whatever illness she had, would miraculously be gone overnight and Rosie would be renewed as the vibrant, powerful, woman she was. I knew; I was fooling myself hiding behind a thin vale of self deceit.

Looking back, my lunch with Rosie was a lunch from hell. The enthusiasm that I had over my new apartment burst, like the air from a punctured helium balloon, leaving me with a sick empty feeling in my stomach. I also felt as vulnerable as I had ever had, even more so, than my first evening in Boston where I initially felt I made the most foolish decision of my young life. As for my expectations for today, as they sometimes say in Viroqua, "The shine seemed to come off the apple". The great joy that I had experienced just that morning seemed to fade with the cold crisp biting wind resonating from the Charles River, as I walked the foot path, that paralleled Storrow Drive. In reality, it was way too cold for a walk but I didn't care. I watched with disbelief, the number of joggers, bicyclists and skateboarders who launched themselves on the cold concrete pathway, and joined me. After an hour or so, I raced back to my apartment in search of a little respite. Bostonians, much like Wisconsinites, are indeed hardy people, or then again, perhaps foolish, for living where we do. I thought my day could not have been worse. Riding an emotional roller coaster, I was looking to frame the remainder of it with as much positive energy as possible, so I decided not to return to my apartment but rather to take in the new contemporary art exhibit showing at the Boston Museum of Fine Arts. If there was one thing that I loved about Boston, it was that unlike Viroqua, it provided an endless amount of diversity and culture, which was open to those who were interested, for a token fee or the student advantage of paying nothing. I had decided very early upon my arrival, that I would try to break through my limited knowledge of the world and expand my horizons with all that Boston had to offer. I would think Rosie would have been proud that I made such a decision. I just couldn't get her off my mind.

I was walking now at a hurried pace, the cold now getting the better of me as the icy wind pushed me back on my heels. *No*, it couldn't be. But it was. *No*, I again said to myself, as I hid in an alcove getting a clearer perspective of him as he walked by. From my better un-obstructed vantage point I could not now deny it. Undoubtedly it was Marc. He looked the same. It had only been a short five months or so, since I last saw him, covered with Chinese food, wrestling on the floor with the waiters at the Golden Dragon. No that wasn't the last time. I corrected myself. It was when the police arrived and I saw Marc being taken away in handcuffs and put in a Boston police cruiser.

If there was anyone I didn't want to see again it was Marc. I was really amazed I would see him walking the streets, thoroughly believing he was in jail and out of my life forever. Why would I be surprised? If there was any-thing I had learned in Boston, it was to expect the unexpected. Initially when arriving in the city, I was caught up in its energy and followed along where it took me. I found just a year later, I was now becoming my own woman., and was beginning to doubt or at least question what presented itself initially as the obvious. I was now totally trying to take the reins of my life and direct them where I wanted to go. Where it would eventually lead me I wasn't sure but one thing I was certain, it as far away from Marc as possible.

After Marc passed by, I again took pause. My respite destination changed. I no longer had the desire to go to the art museum, nor was I stimulated to go back to my new apartment. For some reason I was very much compelled to go back to the Pollards, and found it very strange wanting to return to my place of work on my day off. I decided to just go for it, let my life take me where I needed to go and stop trying to psychoanalyze myself . Just go with my gut. I grabbed the reins. Off to Pollards I went.

I WANT YOU TO HELP ME KILL MY HUSBAND

I walked into the restaurant to the amazement of the bar staff. It were questioning why in the world would I be within ten miles of Pollards on my day off? It hadn't a clue (neither did I) other than I needed to get myself into some familiar surroundings.

Toby Q was the first person I met as I entered the bar.

"Got your calendar messed up, missy?"

"No, not quite," I answered.

"Well, today's your day off. Am I mistaken?"

"No you're dead right."

"Then why the hell are you here? People might begin wondering about you. Spending your time off by being here isn't really a sane thing to do. Some will definitely question your state of mind."

"Screw them. Let them question. I really don't give a damn."

"Well, it might be in the stars."

"Meaning?"

"Meaning, we might be one bartender short tonight."

"And why is that? Is someone sick?"

"Well, that depends how you define sick?"

"Well I can't define anything with just half a story."

"It's Duchess."

" Is she ill?"

"Like no. Well maybe. I don't know what's really going on with her but she's in the office with Peter."

"Why's she there?"

"She came to work pretty banged up. The usual makeup she wears couldn't hide her bruises this time. She looks like someone kicked the crap out of her and she was shaking like a leaf."

"I couldn't believe what I was hearing. Duchess beaten up again, this day was getting progressively worse. What I scheduled as a day of celebration was now going strongly negative, from bad to worse. From worse to God knows where?

"So what you're saying is, she won't be working tonight."

"There's no way in hell Peter would let her work the bar looking like she does. I would say, if you want to stick around and work tonight, I think Peter would be agreeable."

I thought about it for about a minute. I'll work, well that is, I'll hang around and see if it was o.k. with Peter. This was a day I wanted to see come to an end. My working might just occupy my thoughts so I wouldn't be thinking about Rosie, Marc and now Duchess, whom I had not seen, other than her image silhouetted through the thin office blinds.

Several minutes later Duchess came out of the manager's office, accompanied by Peter. She looked terrible. I could see the welts around her eyes. No makeup in the world, could disguise the trauma to her face. I was amazed Duchess showed up for work looking like she had been victimized by a brutal assault. I felt sorry for her as she stood shaking, being escorted out of the office by Peter, who quickly released her arm and walked towards me.

"I'm surprised to see you Nora, am I mistaken or isn't this your day off."

"No, you're not mistaken. It's my day off but for some reason I was drawn to be here tonight."

"Well, whatever brought you here is your concern. Mine, is operating this bar. You want to work tonight? Unfortunately, it seems, we might be one bartender short."

"Sure, why not? I'm here. And like, if you need my help, like I think you might yeah, I'm available."

"Great!"

Peter turned and looked at Duchess.

"And regards to you young lady. It's out of here for you until you get your domestic shit in order. Life's not fair and I damn well know you've been wronged, but I'm running a business here and I can't have all this personal shit spill over negatively affecting it."

Peter walked away, leaving Duchess who walked behind the bar to get her things. I followed close behind, feeling as sorry as I had for Rosie a short few hours before. I addressed Duchess.

"What happened to you?"

Distraught, she answered.

"Like I said a few nights back, my life is a living hell. I'm a caged animal and there is no way I can escape my husband. I've considered calling the cops but if they ever showed up at my door and Roydon was set free, he would come after me, and there would be no telling what he might do."

"Well, what are you going to do about it? And for God's sake why would you ever show up for work looking and feeling like you do?"

"Nora, it's one thing to be an abused woman. It's quite another to be an abused poor one. If I don't work, I don't eat. My good-for-nothing husband besides being all the shit things he is, is also a lousy provider. He hasn't worked for the last year and a half and that's probably where some where some of his anger comes from. But I have to be fair, It's not that he hasn't been looking. I can attest to the fact that he has or I think he has. Well, anyway, that's what he tells me ."

"And you believe him?"

"I have to believe in something to give me hope."

"Duchess, I really wish there was something I can do to help you. Honestly I do. And as much as I want to, I just can't figure a way out for you unless you take charge of your own life. I mean I can help you the best I can, but can't be of any help unless you design a plan for yourself and commit to follow through with it."

"I understand, but .... "

"Yeah, but what? I mean there's got to be someone or some agency out there that can help you."

"Nora, you're so country innocent, but in my case, you might have it right. No, there 's no white knight who is going to come riding in and going to save me. As you said, It all comes down to me. What I will tolerate and what I will do to free myself from the nightmare I'm living. So do you really want to help me or are you just talk? Nora, I mean do you? *Do you? Do you?*"

"Duchess, you damn well know I do. I'm the only person around here who has tried to reach out to you."

"Really, are you sure? Will you help me with the gruesome task at hand?

Duchess's face becomes ghoulish.

"Wow, Duchess, you're now beginning to scare me. What is it that you are asking?

"I want you to help me kill Roydon."

I couldn't believe what I was hearing. Am I really involved in a conversation about murder or am I imagining all this? I mean is this for real?"

"Duchess, do you know what you are asking me? I mean, you're asking me if I will help you kill your husband?"

"You said you'd help."

"Yes help is one thing. Murder is another"

"Well then, I guess your answer no."

"Of course it's no. I can't imagine myself contemplating it, let alone doing it."

"Then I guess I'll just have to kill him myself."

Looking into Duchess's eyes I was damn well sure she meant what she said. She turned quickly and walked towards the restaurant's front door.

"And damn it, you know what makes it worse.?"

"No, Duchess, what?."

"I'm pregnant"

THE DEAD ZONE

Trevor and I conspired to meet on our regular Thursday night. After our shift ended at eleven, thirty p.m. and we cleaned and set up the bar for the luncheon crew, we went to his apartment, where we had unbridled sex well into the early morning. I was going to places I'd never been and honestly couldn't get enough of. I was amazed I felt no shame. There was a distant memory of an innocent girl back in Viroqua, whom I remotely resembled but as I looked into the bathroom mirror, she faded with each passing day.

I was now not only an ultra-promiscuous girl, who'd lie down on a promise, but I was also addicted to a medicine cabinet of drugs ranging from simple blow (pot) to free basing the mother of all escapes, heroin. It wasn't my intention, to get addicted. Whose is?. It happened over the last year, I was living in Boston. A little here, a little there, just a hit, a taste, a brisk encounter with the devil himself. Now I couldn't party without the stuff. It was like my other self had control of my life. Unfortunately, what started as an enhancement to my party girl life was now an essential for me to make it through the day. I was well into addiction but consciously tried to keep myself from acknowledging this. The center of my life now was sex and drugs; everything and all the things my archangel Rosie warned me against.

I didn't need an excuse to rationalize my behavior, I was now into the blame game. Nothing going on with me was my fault. I blamed it on Marc and Trevor, and every other guy I had laid with over the past year. They did this to me, all the bad boys in my life, rendered my innocence invalid. They teased me, preyed on me, screwed me, tweaked me, into the anti-Nora Bergman, my unbridled ugly sister who was dragging me deeper into the maelstrom of the uncontrollable.

I knew what I meant to Trevor and also that there was no future in this relationship. He looked at me as just one of his stable of girls I looked at him as this beautiful guy, who played very much into my sexual fantasy. I was now, or I thought myself to be, a big city girl, and contrary to my rural and limited upbringing, I was looking to get as much sexual experience as I could, as quickly as I could. Buy the scale of things, I felt I was doing all right. I was a diva on training wheels, willing to go and push the limits of who I could be; - Nora Bergman, Midwest Viroqua girl unleashed. Perfect, yes perfect. *Bugga. Bugga, Bugga Booo!*

One major thing that disturbed me about my relationship with Trevor was there was just sex and nothing more. He was the most one-dimensional person I had ever known. He spoke of nothing but himself. Three months into our relationship he had asked me almost nothing of consequence other than where I was from and what had brought me to Boston. I often wondered what kind of person Trevor really was, as he paraded his "wonderfulness" around like a peacock in a pen of peahens.

There was no doubt our sex was great. Unlike a year ago I now had a lot to compare it with other than Marc (and more than a few one night indulgences with a stable of other guys) and the weirdness with Sylvia. Marc was a whole different kind of lover from Trevor I vaguely recalled. Being I never could remember having sex with him other than both of us drinking or stoned. It was just something we dove into after our high. Something that was part and parcel of the whole alcohol, and drug experience. Looking back, I honestly couldn't remember much of it. The majority of it was just haze, elusive memories of us conjoining, two bodies rolling over each other as if it was some kind of absurd Greco - Roman wrestling. In retrospect, it was just weird and whether the majority of it ended, as I thought sex should, with some kind of expulsion, relief or calm, I could not remember either; only that our "high" got in the way of clearly enjoying the moment, as we constantly had to position ourselves in our wet and tangled sheets. We definitely had no clarity of mind, therefore making our co-joining the clumsiest of events.

As distant as my memory was about our physical togetherness, when it did end at least there was some kind of conversation. As foolish and stupid as our bantering sometimes was, at least there was a inkling. It was never overly cerebral. However I do remember having several conversations about life and death. We once discussed the things people immediately turn to once they hear a family member or friend, or for that matter anyone within their sweet circle (we are all seven times removed from one another in one form or another, therefore we must all have a collective soul) becomes ill or died.

"Why do you think that people immediately have sex after someone dies?" Marc had asked me.

"I never knew that. Where did you get that?"

"Read it. Heard it. It doesn't matter. But I guess it's true."

"Well, like I don't know. I never really thought about it."

"Well, you will now."

"Meaning?" as I wiped the sweat from my brow.

"Meaning, well how many ill people have you known.? Then again, how old are you now?"

"Twenty - four."

"Well there you have it. At twenty-four, you shouldn't have experienced a lot of death. Therefore you haven't experienced the thought process death brings you to."

"And how old are you?"

"Thirty - four."

"And like you're saying, ten more years, like makes you an authority on this subject."

"No damn authority, but I bet I've seen a whole lot more death than you have. I've seen what they say, it play out"

"Yeah, sure. Where?"

"Iraq."

"I never knew you were in Iraq."

"You never asked."

"And you never volunteered."

"It's something I never cared to talk about."

"You're talking about it now."

"No, I'm not. I just mentioned it."

"Well, tell me about it?"

"No. Other than this, when soldiers are killed on the battle field the first thing a survivor asks is *"Why wasn't that me?"*

"Yeah?"

"And the second thing is he seeks out as quickly as he can anything that makes him feel more alive, and sex is at the top of that list. In Iraq, and I guess every war that ever took place, soldiers immediately have two choices. Number one, is to heighten their life experience, and the other, quite to the contrary is to dull it with alcohol and drugs. And it is ironic that as opposite as they are, together they're the prescription of choice."

"And what about you?"

"I've tested these waters"

"And what did you find?"

" I found that whether in war or in love, there is a dead zone. In war it doesn't need a expansive explanation. War is hell. Nobody speaks otherwise. Love is another matter. I may not be as evident to others, but in most relationships, many times a black hole exists nonetheless.

"And us?

"We fall into that latter as well."

"You mean ..... ?"

"I mean most of the time between two people there is dead zone, where the relationship is stuck. It beckons us. in fact more than that. It screams out to be heard that the relationship is taking a turn for the worst. In many cases, the relationship will not survive the downward spiral. But sometimes, it can be saved, if there exists on both sides, the desire to save it."

"And what do you say? Are we in that dead zone?"

"Yeah, like I said, almost every couple will be in it, one time or another. It's just a period of reckoning, like two people looking in a mirror and deciding whether one or both want to stay together anymore. Whoa, we're getting way too heavy here. Let's just get high again and screw."

That conversation was the longest and most serious I ever had with Marc. I wrestle with his words everyday, as I try to figure out how I fit into our relationship and how he sees it as well. It took me several more months before I figured out Marc and I did have that "dead zone", that distant separation between us that would always be there and would never be bridged, but it was because that dead zone existed within him. I wasn't sure at first but then the more time I spent with him and the closer I got, that is, the closest he'd let me get, I saw that indeed Iraq had taken its toll. Marc had this bottomless moat around him. He called it a "dead zone" I called it a moat, a wall of armor, an insecurity that he only let partially go, like he would shed one piece of clothing but never fully undress to reveal his naked self.

Yes, my relationship with Marc was far from ideal and the more he drank and drugged, the more he revealed himself as a man in serious pain and the more abusive and dangerous he got. Then there was Trevor.

As experienced and worldly Marc was about life, being I assumed as a soldier in Iraq, whether he wanted to or not, would gain a world pf experience by just being there, Trevor was not. As deep and introspective as I believed Marc wanted to be but could not be, Trevor's life was void. He was that young fresh model looking guy every young girl desired to cuddle up with. As each saw herself as the beautiful queen on the stage, she saw herself on Trevor's arm. He was the perfect man from afar, tall and slender, with a mane of dark brown hair, aquiline features, and dark-green eyes. He was nothing if not alluring. A closer look painted another picture. He was as shallow as a one inch pond, or the gold coating on a lead coin. Trevor didn't play at being ignorant, selfish and thoughtless, he was. As he saw himself as the center of the universe, he saw no one else as consequential, just pages to be folded back in his book of life, or castaways who would be cut away at sea, as his lifeboat only had supplies and essentials for one.

Trevor's personality was as thin as the walls in a Motel 6. There was just nothing there, but then there was the sex. As conceited, self absorbed and shallow as he was, I was still drawn to him because yes, there was the sex and I saw Trevor as an important step on my ladder of sexual exploitation. And now having Marc to compare Trevor with, sex was now more of a existential exercise rather than just a physical indulgence.Unlike Marc, Trevor and I never were drank or drugged when we lay. Truthfully, there never was enough time. By the time we reached his apartment on a Friday morning, after working our shift we were exhausted, but not so much that we could not copulate, which we did over and over again, well into the early hours of the morn- ing. Again, unlike Marc, I had a clear idea of what I was doing and a succinct memory of the many times we lay together. While Marc was a distant memory, like driving lights on a foggy road, just barely enough to navigate the path, Trevor was here and now, real in the most physical sense. I could touch him, feel him, taste him, but after the sex, there was nothing. Nada. Not a blessed thing.

When the sex was completed, Trevor would close down like a clam, not a bloody word, not an utterance, a growl, a whim or wheeze. Again nothing. Within min- utes he would be asleep, snoring his beautiful head off, which I assumed would be a world of admiration he built for himself. He had no time to melt together a single thought with a word or a series, to lay over me like a warm blanket. No, with Trevor, what was done was done and there was no need to establish it in any other way than what it truly was. And it was not anything more than he just screwing me, and me doing the same to him in return.

Many a night, I just lay in his bed, my eyes wide open, letting my imagination run wild, knowing there were several girls before me this week and several would come after and what the hell was I doing here, giving the better part of myself up for hardly nothing, not even a decent conversation, a minimal give and take.

I thought about Marc on the streets again. I hope he wasn't looking for me. The last episode with him, I was involved, scared the hell out of me. I was damn sure he PTS'd out. I've been told war does that to a soldier, and Marc's constant drinking and drugging reinforced the fact he was hiding from someone or something, probably that "dead zone" within himself, the one he was so feverishly speaking he saw only between two people, that in every one as we stand alone, very much exists in everyone.

It was about 11.00 a.m. on a Friday morning as I left Trevor's apartment, I saw Dennis walking into the building. It hit me like a lead shroud. It was so very evident I just didn't see it. I wondered why Dennis was speaking so cautionary about me getting too close to Randolph. He saw me, as I am sure, he saw the other waitresses as a threat to his relationship. Trevor was dipping his pen in all the company ink. I couldn't help but laugh at my naivete, my blatant ignorance. It was so obvious my lack of awareness caused me to shutter. Nora Bergman was still that innocent, naive, country girl from Viroqua. I was now again questioning whether I would survive the big city. It was rolling over me like a blanket of tar.

JINGLE BELLS

I hadn't seen Jimmy Jingles for several weeks now, not that I was concerned but definitely curious. As conspicuous as he was in his dress, he was surely missed and not too few of the regular patrons asked if I had seen him lately being he stood out at the bar like a snow owl in the desert.

We bartenders were in a quandary. Pollards didn't seem like the usual place without Jimmy hanging around anchoring the bar in his maroon suit. Although not very verbose, his just being there added a usual swatch of color.

Rosie was right again. She had to be the smartest person I had ever met. As if scripted *(then they'll come back to you at the bar to see what secrets they exposed in their drunken state)* Jimmy made his appearance three and a half weeks later. He just walked in at his usual 5.00 p.m. hour and strutted right up to his personal bar stool (so he thought), perching himself on it, it seemed he 'd not been absent for the three plus weeks but rather the usual routine unfolded, building on the familiar. He sat quiet for a few minutes and after focusing on the bar menu, raised his arms and spoke in his fragmented, less than dramatic voice.

"Nora, a Gimlet here."

"Sure Jimmy ." I just couldn't refrain from asking, "Where have you been? We haven't seen you for a while"

"Here and there, nowhere special."

"We'll, you've been missed."

The question caused Jimmy to raise his eyebrows. I could see a deep crease between his eyes starting to stress to the max, with one giant life-blood vein now bulging from his temple. There was no doubt I struck a nerve.

"Missed by who?"

"By, like everyone."

" Like everyone, like me, Peter and such and a few, if not more of the regulars have been asking about you."

"Really?" Jimmy responded.

"Yeah, I guess that maroon suit you wear, attracts attraction."

"Yeah, well I like it. In fact, I have several."

"Thank God for that" I thought to myself. I often wondered when and if he ever had it cleaned, if indeed, it was the only one he had. Now I knew and was pleased he wouldn't smell the bar out."

I served up the Gimlet. Jimmy had gulped it down and ordered another by the time I served a patron at the opposite end of the bar. I said to myself, *Christ, here it goes again, Jimmy whacking himself out, please God not again.*

Two Gimlets later, Jimmy was slurring his words and it was a reminder I might be over serving, hanging myself over the edge again. I decided to shut Jimmy off after his fourth drink, which was way over the limit I set for anyone else.

It was about a half an hour later, Jimmy, finished his drink and I was about to drop the hammer on him when he asked me to come closer and again, extend myself over the bar. I couldn't believe this was happening again but I felt I had better humor him because I decided his last drink, was his final drink. I was going to ring the bell on Jimmy Jangles. I had no choice.

Again on my tip-toes I pulled myself as close as I could. Jimmy reached over as well.

Jimmy, in a soft voice.

"Nora, do you remember the last time I was here like a couple of weeks ago?"

"More like three an a half, going on four."

"Well, whatever, three weeks, four no matter, you remember right?"

"Ya, Jimmy, I remember, you were a little shit-faced, in fact, if I can be blunt, a bit more than you are now, but not far off."

"Well anyway, no matter, do you like, remember what I said to you or rather what our conversation was about?"

Rosie, Rosie, Rosie, you're the smartest person on earth. It is just as you said it would be. Jimmy was now back tracking, seeing if he had indeed said something that he shouldn't have said, something that opened his life up to me and created a lot of exposure for him. The little I knew held little relevance for me, other than the incoherent ramblings of a drunk.

"Did I say anything interesting?"

"Interesting meaning what, Jimmy?"

"Meaning, things perhaps you would never think I would say."

Like, stealing something from the "whatever their name" brothers.

I wanted to say.

Rosie was standing on my right shoulder and whispering in my ear (or I thought she was) and she was saying, "You heard nothing. You say nothing."

"I don't recall you saying anything Jimmy!"

"Nothing,?"

"Yes, nothing. Not a blessed thing."

"Like nothing, not a thing worth hearing or ever repeating."

"Jimmy, I don't know what you're fishing for, but rest assured, if you said something important or improper to me, I certainly would tell you, being you seem to be so fixated on it."

Jimmy pushed back on his barstool. I leaned back on my heels, not before I stretched my hamstring. It's going to be a long night with a bad wheel. Damn it. I hated Jimmy for this.

"Well, it's all good then."

"It's all good then."

"Really, you're quite sure now?

"Jimmy, how many times do you want me to repeat myself?"

"So really, nothing was said you might think was out of line?"

"Nothing."

"Then I'll go with that Nora."

Jimmy looked me in the eye. It was a look that told it all. Whatever he was scared of, it owned him heart, mine and soul.

Now that the banter was over, I felt it was my duty (being I was so derelict managing Jimmy drinking his last several visits) to tell him I was shutting him off."

"Jimmy, I'm glad we had our little talk. I really don't know what your trying to find out, but what I told you, is all I know. This being said, you inhaled four Gimlets in less than two hours, and it's not going to take you to a place I feel secure, so, Jimmy, my boy, unfortunately I'm shutting you off."

Jimmy looked at me with his big bloodhound eyes. They were dilated and Easter egg pink, confirming he was already one tote over the line.

"Nora, I don't know what you're doing to me, but this is the second time in a row you've cut me off, and I'm in dire need of several more drinks."

"Jimmy. not on my watch. Look here. You've been over-drinking and frankly, I've been over-serving and that's the truth of the matter. We both are to blame here, so before someone gets hurt or fired, the hurt being you and the fired, being me, we have to do what's right and rational and that's for you to stop drinking and me, to stop serving. That's just the damn way it is."

"Ok., Ok., Nora, I get it but if you know what I'm going through, you'd understand."

"Jimmy, I really don't want to know."

I now wanted to push back on Jimmy and get him out the bar. His constant bantering and drunkenness was sure to catch up with us and I felt we were running out of time.

'Well Nora, I damn well know when I'm not wanted so I'm leaving and whether you know it or not, this may be the last time you'll ever see me."

"Well, I very much doubt that Jimmy, but hoping within the next several minutes, it will be the last time I see you to night."

Jimmy now gets off his stool. He adjusts his suit and starts heading for the front entrance of the bar. Stopping, he then turns around and makes his way back towards me ...

"I'm in big trouble Nora. I know you know. I damn well do. I got a feeling you'll never see me again."

I was now getting really pissed off.

"And, how the hell would I ever know?"

"I'll send you a message Nora, Yes, I'll damn well will find a way to send you one."

A THIEF AMONGST US

Weird things were going on at Pollards. Money was missing. Another one of Rosie's rules was broken. They were falling like duck pins. It seemed multiple times, the receipts didn't balance out with the register at checkout. There was no doubt someone was stealing, but who?

In total there were nine of us, including waiter staff and bartenders, each looked at the others with suspicion. It was incongruous to me how any of the wait staff could be involved, being they had limited or no access to the register. How any of them could was beyond me but with Peter, the restaurant manager, the specter of blame fell over all of us

It was a Tuesday afternoon, when Peter called an emergency staff meeting. Being unusual it put every one on edge. The majority of us thought, business being as bad as it was, (the overall economy was crashing, and an expense easily taken out of a family's budget, was eating out). It was obvious the number of tables being served each night was falling off. The bar however, was still relatively busy, being in bad times, or good times, drinking was the exercise of choice. It was some wanted to celebrate their good fortune. while others drank in remorse or regret. Regardless all nine of us needed a job and the idea of losing ours was terrifying.

Walking into the Peter's office was like walking up to a judge's chambers to have a sentence handed down to us It didn't matter if any of us were guilty. It was rather we had the net of blame thrown over us and since for the most part, we all were basically living paycheck to paycheck, with little if any emergency funds to sustain us, any misfortune or bad luck at all, would throw us over the edge into the dark abyss.

Peter told us that one if not several of us, had crossed that critical line. Thievery in the restaurant business was a cardinal sin, and possibly the worst affront to an establishment and would not be and could not be tolerated. He was incensed with rage.

"This is a very sad day .... in fact one I hoped I would never have to experience in my career but unlike other small infractions, that can be overlooked - STEALING CAN NOT BE."

Each of us knew the seriousness of the accusation the tremor in Peter's voice spoke volumes.

"For those of you who are unfamiliar with God's Ten Commandments, which into days secular world, is probably all of you. It is written THOU SHALL NOT STEAL. My dear people, Pollard's Crab Shack money is not yours. It is one thing to find a dollar on the floor and put it in your pocket and another to try to siphon a percentage of tips from the pot that you are not entitled to, that has sometimes, been overlooked, but stealing from the receipts, from the register cannot be, nor will be tolerated. It is an assault on the business and as one observer so crassly put it, "YOU DON"T SHIT WHERE YOU EAT" I started shaking. I had never seen Peter so riled up. His voice started breaking. His face turned beet red. I thought he was going to pop the vein in his forehead that pulsed

as his voice ebbed and flowed. I had never heard him swear which in the restaurant business is not uncommon. Swearing is second nature to breathing. It is a requisite of employment. Peter however never seemed to have the need. He was always a gentleman and although speaking with authority always had a command of the situation. I had never seen him be anyone other than who I had experienced him but now I was seeing another side, one I really wish I hadn't seen.

"Ladies and gentlemen, you now know I take this infraction very serious and the reason is I predicate my entire relationship with my employer Pollack Carb Shack Corp and those working under me, and that's you. That foundation, and mark my words, is trust. If I can't trust my staff, then I can't trust my life as it unfolds before me. What I want and will make no excuses for is that I must trust you, implicitly. I cannot have any doubts, therefore I must have people with integrity, who I can trust. Trust and integrity go hand and hand. You cannot have one without tother. Integrity is what a person does when no one is looking. You can see that there is a major lack in today's world. Integrity and trust, there is definitely a lack of. I ask you, can you trust your government? Can you trust your friends? Isn't it interesting today, that there seems to be no right or wrong? The only wrong is when someone is caught in an indiscretion and then it seems to take a really serious turn."

'Now, I damn well know I'm being long winded here and the reason is I'm just really disappointed and my ramblings are just my way of coming to terms with it, just my way of working it through. As Obama, our esteemed ex-President would say, *This is a teaching moment.*"

Listening to Peter, my brow was pasting some sweat. I could feel the beads furrowing through my hairline, and an occasional rogue, finding its way to the channel of my back where it rolled through the contour like a sled in a snowy mountain track. As I scanned the others in the room, I could see them glistening under the light. They were nervous as hell. We all shared the same trepidation. The shit was hitting the fan here and I was feeling really insecure as I heard my gastric juices gurgle through my system.

I damn well knew I didn't steal anything and was really upset at the person who did. It was now not about him or her, but rather all of us because we were now "guilty by association". I really hated being put in the same barrel and reflected on something my father said a very long time past, "*One rotten apple can spoil the whole barrel.*" Peter took a deep breath and then started speaking again.

"Now we're not talking about a lot of money here. It's a couple of hundred dollars and no more, but whether it's a dollar or a million, the essence of stealing is still what it is, and you can color it anyway you want, but a pig with lipstick is still a pig, and a person who steals one blessed cent is still a thief. Do you understand me here?"

We all nodded yes in unison. "*O.k., you all get the gist of my disappointment? If so then here is where the rubber meets the road. This is now the moment of truth, where the person or persons who stole the money must identify themselves. If there is any redemption here, it must begin with the truth, so I'm asking in the most straight forward way to resolve the issue so we all can determine where we go from here. I am now looking at my watch and the window is one minute. Yes, the guilty person or persons has but one minute to redeem themselves and free all the others from the specter of being a thief. It is critically important to know that in the food and beverage business, there is no room for crooks and liars. As large but as knit as this business is, word gets around quickly and therefore if this matter is not resolved to my satisfaction, I dear say, all of you, yes, every single one will carry the stigma and will find little if any employment available, once I let the word out."*

"Holy Shit", I heard myself saying to myself. I couldn't believe this was happening to me. I stole nothing nor had any idea of anyone stealing from Pollard's. I looked around at my fellow workers and saw them all looking around as well. They all seemed frightened and upset, some more than others, but each was showing visual discomfort.

If I don't keep this job there is no way to support myself. It will be impossible to keep my apartment and recover from there. I couldn't get the thought out of my head that my adventure In Boston might be coming to an end. I was mortified and hoped the culprit, who-ever he, she or they are, will quickly step forward, One minute later, still nobody did.

Peter, in his most disparaging tone; *"To say, I am disappointed, is an understatement. For the responsible party, you know you are putting all your fellow workers in harm's way. Well, it is what, it is - and the results of this façade, will in time, speak volumes. As with any indiscre-tion, there will be a price to pay, and it will be paid now or later, obviously, from what has transpired - it will be into the future, but mark my words, it will be paid. From this moment on, you are all on notice, meaning you are*

now walking on eggshells, the floor under you is shat-
tered and fragile and any indiscretion will be your last.'
I really didn't know what to do from here, so I decided
to continue my routine as if non-interrupted. Hopefully,
whoever it was who exposed the staff, would eventually
"belly up to the bar" and make everything right, then I
began to think ,Why the hell would they? What's in it for
them, nothing, and nothing means you have everything
to lose but to what purpose? Two days later everything
had changed at Pollards. There was now an air of suspicion that fell over us like a circus tent in a hurricane.
Weighty by its nature , it allowed no frivolity, or ease
of purpose. Everyone was skeptical of each other. The
"free to be me" bantering that brought a social climate
to our workplace was gone. Free flowing words were a
scarcity. Everyone, except the thief, I would believe was
thinking the same thing. "How the hell can anyone steal
and then lay the consequences on the shoulders of the
whole staff. Then like an oasis in the desert, *I answered*
myself, "because they are a thief and it goes along with
an absence of character ..... that's how.

A DAY FROM HELL

It was a day from hell.. I had never felt so exposed. I wanted to cry but just couldn't allow it. Bergman's don't cry. We were from Viking heritage. We died with our swords in our hands or I thought we did. Vikings, however, only had to worry about wielding their sword and fighting and dying for Thor, they didn't experience the humiliation of being called out as a liar and thief, or the exposure of being a twenty-four year old girl, on the verge of being penniless, unable to pay her rent, possibly being put out on the street. Vikings also never returned to their home fires with their tail between their legs, in retreat from their desire and dreams. If indeed, I had a choice, I would rather experience a Viking's death but then again, here I stood.

I left the Pollard's as stressed as I could be. Thoughts swam around in my head almost bringing me to frenzy. I felt like I had ingested three cups of Starbucks coffee. There wasn't a rational thought in my head and as if I was deserving of the cruelest of days there he was. He tried to hide from me but I caught just a glimpse of him as I crossed Boylston Street. Hiding in an alcove, he was a bit more visible than he thought. I then saw him step out of the doorway, as I ungracefully maneuvered through traffic, trying to get to the other side of the street. Before I knew it, he was in my face.

"Bitch!"

"Marc. I thought you'd be in jail."

"And I damn well know you would have really liked that."

"No, I'm just surprised, that's all. I mean, like the last time I saw you, you were handcuffed and being dragged away by the police."

"And that's just it you bitch. After that I never saw or heard from you again."

I didn't like where this conversation was going. It was getting really testy and I wasn't in the mood. I tried to step around Marc and continue my journey, to who knows where? Marc blocked my movement and with a stiff right hand pushed me back several feet. It was a flight or flight moment and before Marc could react I was running down the sidewalk, with him in hot pursuit. I made it maybe fifty yards before he caught up with to me. Grabbing my jacket, it felt like he ripped my shoulder from its socket. I tripped and fell to the ground. I could feel the flesh burning, as I scraped my kneecap on the asphalt. I was down, Marc was on top of me and grabbing my hair, tried to drag me to the parking garage, not ten yards away. I was hoping some one would come to my aid but it was quarter past midnight. and there was no one in sight. I was scared senseless I was going to die but just like that Marc loosened his grip and he was gone. A quick survey of my surrounding told me why. The cruiser turned towards me and put on its siren and running lights. Before I knew it, I was in the car being interrogated by two metro policemen,"

"So Miss, why were you on the ground?"

What the hell could I say. I was terrified Marc, would come back after me if I squealed on him. The Marc I just met was an animal, full of rage (and I hadn't a clue way), what would he be like if he ever knew I betrayed him?

"I just slipped that's all". I was visibly shaken.

"Do you need to go to Mass General to get checked out, we'll take you there." the police because, it's best they know Marc is roaming the streets and need to get a read on him, that he was staking me and something they best record.

I came clean and the police took me down to the station. I learned after the incident at the Chinese Restaurant, Mark was held for several months for psychiatric observation. He was determined to be sane but under the influence of opioids and alcohol. He was held under a $10,000 bond and was eventually bonded out by his uncle. (Marc told me, both his parents were dead). Once released the police lost contact with him, being he never showed up for his court date (his foolish uncle, lost his ten grand).

One hour later, I was deadheading to my apartment. My phone rang. It was not unexpected. I knew Marc had my number. Again, I was in a quandary whether to answer it or not. I grabbed the cell and put it to my ear.

"You fucking asshole, what are you doing, chasing me and attacking me like you did?"

"You bitch, you left me behind. You let the cops take me away, just dissed me just like that."

" Marc, you're totally wrong ...... "

Marc's not listening - he interrupts.

"I've been abandoned all my life, you bitch and you threw me away like a piece of shit and you'll damn well pay for it. I know where the hell you live and where you work. and I'll tell you another thing, you damn well better not tell the cops, what happened. if you do, I'll kill you. I damn well mean it, I'll kill you fucking dead."

Marc hangs up,

Shit, I'm screwed. Marc has gone over the cliff. He's insane. I'm scared shit. Unfortunately, I'm all in. As my father used to saw "either fish or cut bait." I reached for my cell.

"Officers, Duffy and McLane, Boston Metro Police. No, its not an emergency, then again - it may be - but I'm not really sure"

I AM NOT A VICTIM

I rose from my bed. My head was full of variations of how my day would play out. Marc entering my life again, was it real or just a residue dreaming of our past relationship? No, it was real. Wanting no part of him now, I felt I had been violated but in true Viking form there would be consequences. When and by what means was another question but that was secondary falling behind my determination to totally remove Marc from my life.

I will not be a victim! I will not be a victim! I will not be a victim! If there was one thing my mother had etched into my head it was that life was determined by a number of choices. Most are small but a few are large as they present themselves. Choices weave the fabric of who we are. *I choose today, not to be the victim but the executor of my whole life, and to free myself from that which does not benefit me.*

The sex with Marc had been great but that was where it ended. After he attacked me, I designated him to be Nora Bergman' enemy number one. How did the bastard violate me as he did? How dare he degrade my being as someone he could wipe the streets of Boston with? His total lack of respect for me grated my inner being. One is not important to anyone, if they are not important to themselves. I had not yet waded into those bottomless dark waters. If there was one thing I had learned in coming to Boston, it was either you empowered yourself or others would roll over you like a lawn mower would over a blade of grass.

You better watch the hell what you are doing, you fucking maggot Marc Mandady because this Bergman, is armed and dangerous. Not knowing how I would arm myself or how dangerous I could be, I assumed myself able and lethal, nonetheless.

Yes, I ratted on Marc, may he rest in hell. Hopefully, the cops will get him back in the cage where he belongs.

I was back at Pollard's. Things there were now getting progressively worse. The person who stole the money (me) wouldn't fess up. I didn't know when or how I stole the money. Why was easy. I was flat broke and the inability to pay my bills wore on me like a blanket of razors, cutting me to my very core.

I remember my father several times schooling me with a saying from an old English playwright, something like *"neither a borrower nor a lender be."* That's why in England, they had debtor's prisons where those who didn't hold dearly to their purse paid dearly for their lack of attention. My father would be mortified, knowing I could no longer pay my bills and was now a felon stealing from my employer. Rosie had also warned me and I let her advice go unheeded as I did with several male co-workers with whom I had shared a bed.

Working at Pollard's was now like working in a freezer. The atmosphere was brutally cold. The absence of trust and comradary made it a terrible place to work. Everyone was waiting for the hammer to fall. What would be the next thing to happen? Who would be fired? who would fess up to stealing the money? No one. No one because I was the one and there was no way in hell I was going to confess. If I did, I would never be able to get future employment in any other bar or restaurant in Boston, or perhaps any place else. I knew my indiscretions would be posted on Facebook, Twitter and Snap-Chat and my name would be like a virus. Nora Bergman, is a thief and a liar. Unemployable. Unemployable. Unemployable.

I stole the money. Yes. I stole it and didn't have the guts to fess up leaving all the other bartenders and wait staff exposed. What a really cowardly thing to do. I hung them all out to dry. What does that make me, a liar, a coward, a buddy fucker. Yes, I was all of these and more, and most unsettling was that just a few years before, I was just a shy young woman who left Viroqua, Wisconsin to grow up and make it in the big city, Boston. So far Boston 1 (or maybe a 100 or perhaps a 1,000), Nora Bergman 0, but I was trying).

The city was rolling over me and squashed me like bird turd in the road. I now questioned myself, *"Will I ever put on my big girl pants and face life straight on, not letting everyone run interference for me.?* Damn it, probably never."* If I didn't face up to what I had done I would never be able to grow up. How had the money gotten into my dresser drawer? I didn't have a clue. I couldn't remember a damn thing. This above all was scaring the living hell out of me.

BATTERED AND BROKEN

"**S**he what?"
"She was battered to death."
"Dead?"
"Yes, her husband finally pushed it to the nines and beat her to death with a hammer."

I couldn't believe what Toby was saying, Duchess was dead.

We all knew it would happen someday. She lived under the most trying circumstances, every night going home to an animal who did nothing other than batter her and her kids. It was bad, we all knew it, but to what extend, we knew now. We should have done something more than what we did. In retrospect we did nothing except occasionally pass judgment on her. I wished I could have helped. Together we could have devised a plan to have killed her husband. I couldn't believe what I was thinking. It couldn't have come from an innocent girl from Viroqua Wisconsin. I was becoming a different person. Boston was chipping away at the core of who I was and revealing now the person, I had grown to be, hard, calculating, bold, a liar and a thief. Why not a killer too? Several days later, coincidentally, I focused on an article in the *Boston Globe* discussing the growing problem of battered women. In the past ten years, there has been thousands of domestic cases in greater

Boston, culminating in 243 homicides and 91 perpetrators deaths committing suicide or being killed by the police.

How many women (and men) went home to intolerable abusive situations was impossible to record but there was no doubt, the number of battered women and children was on the rise.

CAUSES OF DOMESTIC ABUSE;

- Disagreement with their intimate partner
- Protracted periods of unemployment
- Financial issues
- Desperation when partner threatens to leave
- Anger escalation
- Humiliation stemming from problems at work or other perceived failures
- Jealousy and envy .....

And probably a myriad of other .....

I wondered what had caused Duchess's husband to take his wife's life. Can a person get so out of control that the reins of restraint cannot pull him back? When is the next step forward which is the critical factor that there will be no retreat from here, that what must be done, has already been decided? Whether one perceives it to be their fate or not, it is their fate

It was time to see Rosie, my confidante, my confessor. I shuttered at the idea of telling her what I had done. She'd be bat–shit, but I had to tell someone and that someone was my archangel.

LIFE IS UNCERTAIN
AT BEST

I left messages for Rosie but hadn't heard back. I decided against my better judgment to walk over to Clarendon Street and surprise her. Honestly, I was thinking more about myself than the wrath of Rosie. My guilt was breaking through my skin. I was now seeing myself as a restaurant whore, and added to that a liar and a thief.

As a small boat tender needs to be secured against the harsh wind, I needed Rosie's counsel . She had been there before and undoubtedly would be again. She had that one more giving seed. She just had to extend herself for others. It was in her DNA. She just gave a damn.

Life is uncertain at best.

Rosie was gone. There would be no more lessons. No more counsel. No more understanding and guidance. There was no more Rosie and me. Now just Boston and me.

The apartment door just wouldn't open. I'd been knocking on it for several minutes and in between calling Rosie on my cell phone.

Finally an old man came out of his apartment and asked, "You looking for Rosie? I take it you are.

"Yes, I am."

"Gone, last Thursday. Her brother just showed up and took her back to Warren, Ohio, wherever the hell that is. She should have been in a hospital but refused to go. She wanted to stay at home. Hospice visited her everyday in the afternoon. Then her brother shows up unannounced and says to me, that she's going back home where she was raised. He took out what he could from her apartment, wrapped her in blankets, put her in his van and just like that, was gone."

Shit, shit, shit. It was just registering with me. My nearest and dearest is now gone and I felt very alone. I started to feel a big lump in my throat, a tightness in my chest. Sweat started to pour from my brow. I was having a panic attack.

"Are you alright, Lady?" the old man asked.

"Yes, I just need to compose myself."

Minutes later, I was out the door, destination: my apartment. As near as it was, it seemed so far away.

Rosie, you will be forever in my heart.

THE PRACTICED ART OF LYING

"**D**ad ..."

"Yes.?"

' It's me Nora."

I didn't want to but I needed to call. I hadn't spoken to my parents over a month,

As hard as it was then (my just about making it on my own) it now was considerably harder (being I was now finding myself at my wit's end. It was going now on over a year and six months, me living in Boston. Upon my arrival, my hopes were high but days and months have a way of getting away from me and they escaped from my grasp the harder I tried to hold on to them.

My Dad caught up to the anxiety in my voice.

"Nora, are you alright?":

"I'm all right, why yes, I'm fine."

"Well damn it, you don't sound well to me."

I probably shouldn't have called. Who knows better the fabric of a child other than a parent.

"No there's something wrong. I can hear it in your voice."

"NO, what you hear is my Boston accent coming to roast."

"Well, if that's all it is, but I doubt it, I liked the way you sounded before."

"Yeah, Daddy, I imagine you would."

"Yes, I think that big city living is getting the best of you. Your bed is still waiting if you ever decide to move back."

If there was anything I didn't want to hear, it was this. My Dad's words reinforced the fact I wasn't doing well in Boston. As expected, everyone back home thought I would fail, that is everybody but me. There was no way I could let this happen. I would be a disappointment in everybody's eyes and as I was already seeing, I was in mine. I had to divert my Father's attention he was just way too close to that which was breaking me.

"Daddy, is Mommy there?"

"What's with you? You're just gonn'a give your old man a few minutes of your time? Is that all I'm worth?"

"No Daddy, I just want to say hello to Mother that's all."

I couldn't believe how difficult this conversation was going. I called home just to capture a friendly voice, to reassure myself if indeed, my life in Boston went to hell in a handbag I still was welcomed home. I knew my family wished me well, but deep in it's heart of hearts, it wanted me to fail, not that it was a lesson I needed to learn but rather my lack of success would drive me back, to where they believed I truly belonged.

Why my Father's voice weighed on me as it did I didn't know. Maybe it was because, in the strangest way, I felt my leaving brought them the greatest of angst, knowing their little girl (not so little any more at twenty four) rendered them as failed parents. Perhaps they felt my strong need to break away was driven by their great desire to keep me under small town wraps, as close to the nest as possible. Perhaps the culture in Viroqua reinforced that families should stay together because it's truly the natural thing to do, and most families did, but the outlier that I am would not be deterred.

My Father handed the phone to my Mother.

"Nora, It's so nice to hear from you."

"Yes Mother."

"Yes, it certainly has been too long."

Damn it, here comes the guilt again.

"Yes, I'm sorry. I've been caught up in work and all."

"Yes you must be busy."

"Oh, yes Mother I really, really am."

"Certainly getting that hi-falutin job at that law firm and all ..."

"Yes. It keeps me very busy."

"Again, what is it that you do there?"

"Ah, well, like I'm an executive secretary. I coordinate the day to day activities for all the key executives in the office."

"Oh, yeah, like their right hand man."

"Yes Mother, but in this case, their right hand women."

"And are you still with that boyfriend of yours? What's his name?"

"Aaron."

"Yes, are you still seeing him?":

"Yes Mother, I am."

"Well, we would love to meet him. Why don't you bring him home for Thanksgiving or Christmas? He sounds like a nice young man."

Ok, ok, ok, so I'm also a big liar. I have already established that. It was just the easiest thing for me to do. My parents barraged me with questions. I was their little girl and would always be. They tried with the best intentions, to pry into every small detail of my life.

I decided several years back, to mitigate the onslaught, that I would tell them what they wanted to hear, that their little girl, Nora, was doing just great in the big city, in fact was taking it by storm. The red carpet was being laid out for me, that my coming to Boston was pre-empted by a big parade, where thousands showed , banners, horns, confetti and all, just like the ones for the Patriots, after another Super Bowl win.

Yes, I laid it on thick, knowing it made my parents sleep well at night and for me it took a bit of the edge off, knowing this. If this is what they wanted to hear then I served it up. A child has a duty to their parents to at least try to exceed to their expectations and I decided, if success was not warranted, then to bring down the primrose path nonetheless.

The more I thought about it, the more mortified I became. The crap I laid on them was just plain wrong but it was far better than *the truth*. Law firm, bullshit, I was a fucking bartender and the reality, not a very good one. I could bullshit myself but I knew compared to Rosie and Duchess, I was nowhere in their league. I was hired because I was a natural blonde who was amply endowed, sporting a figure that drew men to me like flies to honey. My bartender skills were nothing compared to the fantasies I conjured up in the marinated imaginings of my bar clientele. The males fantasied my being in bed with them, some women as well. My woman patrons, for the most part, saw me as a member of their Ya Ya Sisterhood, one of their sorority sisters, who no matter which side of the bar I worked, knew only that which only a woman can. We are empowered beyond our backsides and boobs, with an incredible instinct for survival that few, if any men could understand. My mother had the gift. Everyone else I ever met (I'll give Rosie an honorable mention here) paled compared to her instinct to teach her children the survival skills needed in a not too compliant world.

I would damn well like to tell her the truth, because I knew she'd understand that a girl's got to do, what I girl's got to do to survive, but my Father and siblings would not understand, so my decision was to spin one story that although dishonest, at least I felt had the right intent.

My conversation with my Mother lasted almost an hour, fifty-nine minutes too long. She tried to pry from me every detail of my life in Boston. She wanted to know everything that unfurled over the last several months. The more questions she asked the more I lied. She damn well knew some things just didn't match up but I tried to cover them up as best I could. There was no doubt her main intent was to find out if I was sharing an apartment and sleeping with my (imaginary) boyfriend. I wanted to tell her I'm sleeping with a lot of boyfriends and an occasional woman too but what the hell would that accomplish making the whole prodigal daughter scenario that much worse.

When I hung up I found myself in a catatonic state looking at the wall. The conversation made me feel just the opposite of what I expected. Instead of getting any solace out of the call, I found myself more at angst. Yes, I was now twenty-four but I was still my parents little girl and there were certain things that a parent expects from their child and one of these is *the truth*. Yes, *the truth,* which I was unable to serve up made me feel I had now gone so far into my lies that I was not able to separate the two realities. A liar I was, A thief as well. I was alcohol and drug addicted to the nines. I was now as promiscuous as I could be. I was now a restaurant whore. It was now my habit that as I changed restaurants, or met new employees, I found myself jumping from one bed to another. How would you like the truth now, Mom and Dad? How would you like *the truth* now?

I FELT ASHAMED AND GUILTY AS HELL!

I STOLE THE
MONEY

I stole the money. I couldn't believe my eyes. How it got there I didn't know. It was like seeing snow in the desert. It made no sense at all. I had no recollection of taking it, in fact, couldn't remember ever entertaining the thought. The reality however, was it was there, in my dresser drawer, wades of bills I had no remembrance of their origin. Living alone, no one else could have put them there but me. I picked up the stash and quickly counted it. The exercise concluded, it was the same denomination as the missing funds at the Shack. I damn well must have stolen them, I damn must have, but not a hint of remembrance. I was losing my damn mind.

Next to the money was my new best friend opiates, vials. It seemed for the last several months they accompanied me more than my shadow. It was a slow progression walking off the cliff. It started with just a taste. Curiosity drove it.

I was told it brought new dimension, insight unattainable under a normal state of mind. It took sex to a new level, enhancing it ten fold, orgasmic to the state of exhaustion. "Hallelujah, Hallelujah. Hallelujah."

I was in a constant frenzy now. I needed money, I needed drugs, I needed sex. Each morning started with the craving, each night ended the same. A complete emptiness, feeling I was just the shell of the person I wanted to be, but after a few pills, washed down with a beer casher, I felt I was the grand princess, the woman I dreamed who had control over her life and the power to impose my intentions on all others. The power I felt brought an awareness and grandiosity only imagined, I was now experiencing exuberant highs and debilitating lows. My life was a roller coaster and I was riding untethered. To hell, knows where.

JIMMY, FROM THE GRAVE

I t was a strange Thursday night, dreary at best. What made it even more so was the over hanging atmosphere at Pollards. No one trusted anyone else any more. There was a thief among us hanging us all out to dry. My secret is that I knew who he was, *it was me,* and I felt so damn tangled up in my T briefs I hadn't a clue how to repair the break in trust we all had. There was no more team work, we all interacted but none of us communicated. We were all looking out for ourselves. The bar and restaurant business is "dog eat dog", especially when there is a thief within its midst. I was in a quandary. I hadn't a clue how to make it right, so I chose to do nothing, cowardly me.

The night as strange as it was, was made even more strange when a florist's delivery man walked into Pollards carrying a bouquet of purple roses. All eyes turned to him.

"Is there a Miss. Bergman here?"

Did he say Miss Bergman?"

It finally registered. It was me.

"Over, here, I'm Nora Bergman."

The carrier walked the roses over to me. I took them, there was a note attached.

It was addressed Miss Nora Bergman.

I separated the note from the flowers and opened it and walked to the back of the bar to read it.

Nora, these purple roses have been sent to you from me Jimmie Jingles from the grave. I told you the last time we spoke that I was in serious trouble and that you would never see me again. These purple roses are a confirmation of that. I knew I made a mistake, in fact, the biggest of my life, and I have paid the dearest price. I did not want you to spend any energy thinking about what happened to me. So now you know.

I ordered these flowers to be sent to you on this day if I thought what was going to happen .... happened, unfortunately, it did. If it did not I would have cancelled the order and would be sitting at your bar ordering a Gin Gimlet .... So please have one in remembrance of me

Enjoy the roses ..... because they like me ....will be dead sooner than you think.

Live well
Jimmy Jingles

I couldn't believe what I was reading. As promised, Jimmy was sending me a message from the grave. I reflected back to the last night we spoke and how scared he seemed to be. As drunk as he was, I must admit I took Jimmy's words with a grain of salt. I always looked at him as part of the bar's dressing, an unusual character who seemed a woeful step out of fashion and time. His presence created a lot of interest and specu-lation. Nobody really knew who he was or what he did. He just threw a lot of banter up in the air and let it fall on those who were the most curious.

I wonder what these people would say if they knew what I knew, if they knew Jimmy was dead.

There was some really scary stuff going down. Reality has no greater impact than the dead reaching out from the grave and touching you. It has been said that things usually happen in threes. Who ever said that, in this instant, he/she was dead on the mark. First it was Rosie, then Duchess, now Jimmie Jingles. There was a lesson here to be learned. I really didn't know what it was, but I knew it was weaved in the fabric of my life. Yes, there was a golden tread of knowledge and wisdom that was waiting for me, if I chose to seek it out. Maybe it is that no matter the path chosen, the common denominator in every-one's life is it will be terminated at one point. Three totally different souls now have been snatched from my life and none of them lived a life that was anyway parallel to mine,

Rosie's life was full of love. She gave to those in need. I admired her for this, however she lived in a cocoon. Duchess lived a life of constant fear, and like a puppy beat into submission by a cruel master, unfor-tunately, did not have the strength or courage to fight back. Then there was Jimmy's Jingles, a flimflam man. Nobody really knew what he did or who he was. He was a mystery to all of us, constantly wearing a purple suit (what the hell was that about), buying drinks for people he didn't know, saying things that made him look larger than who he was as he set the stage to entertain those, as an ambassador of the city he was not. Jimmy would have been better off living in Detroit, the home of Prince and Purple Rain. In Boston he was a fish out of water, the total opposite of what a visitor to this great city would ever expect. Jimmy played at his life but not too well it seems now.

Death made me want to take off the reins, to walk to the edge of the cliff, to get closer than ever before. It made me want to feel more alive, to live full and large. I wanted to have more to drink, to further experiment with drugs (I was well on my way to trying them all) and then having as much sex as I could, with as many varied men and taking my sexual self to places I've never gone before. I wanted to dig my teeth and long nails into flesh and bone and ravage the men I met, as a vulture would pick the meat from the bones of its kill. I wanted to feel alive, not skirting around the periphery of my existence, but rather dining at the table of my life – consuming the whole banquet.

I want it all. I want it all and to tell the world that I was no longer the innocent, naïve young girl from Boston.

VIKINGS DON'T QUIT

I keep getting calls and every time I go to answer, the caller hangs up. There was no name that registered. The longer I stay in Boston, the more paranoid I am becoming. Sometimes I see myself as nothing but a grain of sand, insignificant to others but myself. Other times, I see myself as the entire compass of the universe with everyone and everything rotating around me.

Today I feel the weigh of the world is on my back. I'm weighed down and feel so transparent and that everyone knows my secret (I'm striking out in Boston) but unlike the revered Red Sox, I have never won a conference title, certainly no World Series, not even one game. I've won nothing. My batting average is 00.000 because as I perceived myself, I couldn't even bat in the minor leagues. I will sit on the bench at best.

There was no doubt in my mind, that the city of Boston has pitched a shut out against me. I was now contemplating leaving. I couldn't believe I was entertaining such a thought but I was. This alone very much disturbed me. Nora Bergman, a quitter. No damn way. I'm from Viking heritage. Vikings don't quit. We make the other bastards run for refuge.

The phone rang again. I grabbed it and was prepared to assail the caller dead with my onslaught of profane verbiage but before I could render my tank empty, I heard the voice that rendered me paralyzed.

"Nora, this is Marc. Hear me out before you hang up the phone."

My ear was frozen to the phone in anticipation.

"I'm listening."

"You bitch. You put the cops on me."

"No, you brought them on yourself. It was you who attacked me and not the other way around, and that begs the question, Why? Why? I didn't do anything to you."

"You abandoned me at the Chinese restaurant. You left me high and dry after the cops brought me in. I heard nothing from you. You threw me away like a piece of garbage."

"I don't get it Marc. I mean like what could I have done. I wasn't involved. You were - like melting down. You kept hitting Mr. Kim with a bottle."

"He had it coming."

"Mark, have you lost your marbles? You assaulted him for no reason at all."

"Bullshit."

"Nonetheless, I have no money, no power. There was nothing I could have done to help you. In fact I can't believe you are out of jail and talking to me."

"If it wasn't for my rich uncle posting bond, I damn well wouldn't be. The guys got more money than brains. Lucky for me."

"Unlucky for the rest of the world", I was thinking.

I was getting really nervous. My hands were beginning to sweat Why was Marc calling me? It didn't take long to figure out."

"I'm going to get you Nora. You sold me out to the cops. Now, I'm on the run and I guarantee you, I'm going to get you before they get me."

Marc is deranged. How can he blame me for all the shit in his life? He is an alcoholic and a drug addict (unfortunately now, not unlike me, but to a far greater extent). In fact he was the one who turned me on to what I now believe is the scourge of my life. My drinking and drugging was now too frequent, taking me over. I was now in constant search, all my spare time was chasing drugs or the money to purchase them. If anyone was detrimental to the other, it was Marc to me.

"I'm going to get you Nora. On that you can make book. Somewhere, someday, Some how.'

"Fuck you" and I hung up.

Wow, now I'm not only scared for my job but I'm scared for my life. I had hoped my breaking away from Viroqua would be the best decision of my life. I wanted so badly to sever the chain of restrictive behavior that corralled and stifled me. It was my coming out party, my call to arms, my red chili alarm that my time had come. I now have been in Boston for over a year. My mother used to say to me, *you never know where you're going until you know where you've been.* It was time to re-evaluate, to draw the line of demarcation, to see how I have traveled and to what purpose. I grabbed my cell phone and under notes, I wrote

<u>My Goals</u>

1) To expand my horizons from small town bumpkin to a big city girl.

2) Find a good paying job.

3) To get an apartment of my own.

4) Saving for my future.

5) Expand my mind with mind altering drugs.

6) Explore every aspect of my sexual self

7) To somehow (by hook or crook) get season tickets to the New England Patriots .

Underneath these, I wrote down what I thought I achieved.:

1) Success, I got out of Viroqua. Have I now achieved big city status? Hell no, I was still a country bumpkin.

2) Finding a decent job, I found myself qualified for nothing. I am but a journeyman bartender who doesn't have the skills or resume to command the big bucks. My share of the tips, is disproportionate to the others, who have resumes as long as a roll of toilet paper and who can work the bar like a surgeons. I know I was hired because (honestly) I was a good-looking woman. I know it because I have been hit on all my life. My looks are my trump card and made up for my many short falls most men overlook.

3) My hopes for a nice apartment of my own diminished quickly as prices for even the most minimal space in Boston, escalated beyond my ability to pay. It took me over a year to find anything acceptable (if indeed that meant a below prime studio at the exorbitant rent of $1795 a month.

4) Saving for the future, are you kidding me? I barely make enough money to pay my rent and monthly bills let alone, saving for a future in doubt. Saving

for a rainy day ... The majority of my days are caught up in a shit storm.

5)   In regards to expanding my mind. It is consumed with escaping the burden of my reality as much as I can. I am now ingesting more pills than a pharmacy. Whatever I can get my hands on I was taking. The drugs combined with the alcohol put me in a state of euphoria and/or mild depression. To say that my life is an emotional roller coaster is an understatement.

6)   Exploring my sexual self. If there is anything I deeply regret, it was rolling over for every attractive man I meet. I am like a depleted woman in the desert, trying to capture as much nourishment as I can. Sex and its every variation was laid out as a banquet on my table and I gorged on it. I just can't get enough. The succulence of eating the forbidden fruit attracts me without reservation.

7)   A season pass to the Patriots. I must be kidding. They keep on winning and I keep on losing. A season pass to the New England Patriots – *no way in hell.*

FIGHT OR FLIGHT

Marc was stealing my sleep, my well-being, my life. I became obsessed with him. I knew him too well or perhaps not well enough to render me capable of any reasonable thought. This I knew: Marc was a mad man and I'd be a fool not to heed his warning. I knew he was still alcohol and drug dependent because I was as well and knew as badly as I craved it, he did more.

I was now in constant communication with the police. Once I broke the sacred covenant there was no reason for me not to continue. If Marc was going to try to kill me, then he would try , cops or no cops, so I'd be a fool not to ask for their support. What I soon learned was that I was not the only person being stalked in Boston. There were hundreds, perhaps thousands, and I would have to fall in line.

The calls and threats kept coming. Marc was relentless. He constantly found ways to intimidate me: the prank calls, the threatening notes in my mail box, the dead bird in my stairwell, it was his strategic plan to wear me down. I sometimes thought that he didn't want to kill me but rather to spend his life just threatening me, playing one trump card after another until he drove me mad, which he was well on the verge of doing. I knew I was losing it. I couldn't concentrate at work. I failed to remember the mixture to some of the basic drinks, never mind, the iconics. I stayed in my apartment the majority of the time I was not working. It was my safety zone but I was bored as hell. I found myself drinking and drugging more, and spending the majority of my time a lone, planning how to solicit drugs with the little money I now had, since my tips were getting smaller because I was less engaged. What worried me more was that I lost my interest in sex. Me, Nora Bergman, the undeterred fuck around was not fucking around anymore. Whether it was the alcohol, the drugs or just the plain fear in me, my hormones were no longer in an uproar.

It was now intermittently hearing from Marc and then there would be nothing but darkness for weeks. I hoped he had crawled into his sewer and I would never see him again. Better yet, someone had killed him, or he was in an accident hit by a car, anything to render him fatal. Marc was playing his game well. My thoughts were constantly on him. He was renting space in my head and paying nothing in return. I was taking the brunt of the punishment and finally concluded, being as close to my critical edge as possible, I could not continue to live like this. Some thing had to be done, but the question was what?

I started to think about whether to stay in Boston or throw in the towel and go back home where I probably belonged. After more than a few years in the big city, I had made little headway and honestly had to face the fact that my future wasn't looking bright. I was just (although a Viking blonde) one of thousands of young women romanced by the idea they could break out and become that rogue city girl.

Frankly, I was becoming someone I didn't like. My innocence had now escaped me like a young bird falling from its nest. I was as paranoid as I could be and beginning to see nothing but dark clouds on the horizon. That big blue canopied Boston sky seemed to be lost to me forever. I was now shrouded in darkness.

I began carrying a knife. I would have carried a gun if I was able to get a license, (in Boston, unlike Viroqua, it was not an easy thing to do). Often times, I found myself too scared to go out of my apartment obsessing on all the variables that could happen to a young woman living in semi-seclusion. My hours at work now seemed to be limited. I just didn't have the energy or the desire to work a full shift, and begged off every opportunity to work a double. I was adamant about what I wanted. Management wasn't pleased. Peter looked away but I could see him getting angrier at me by the minute. I knew something was going to come to a head. My life just could not keep going on this way. There was a breaking point and I could see it building on the horizon. At twenty- four years old, my life sucked. I was now scared beyond description.

It was inevitable Marc would find me. His anger kept escalating. I could hear it in his voice when he called. I didn't know why I answered my phone but I was compelled. My mother used to say *"It's best to keep your friends close but your enemies closer"*. I heeded her advice, knowing that someday I would have to deal with him and it was best I got an accurate read.

I didn't see him at first as he hide in the shadows. I was focused on getting through the garage as quickly as possible, I used it to short-cut a couple of blocks to my apartment. It was a foolish decision, one of many I had made over the years, that were now coming at me with a frequency I could no longer control. Every decision I made of late seemed to be misguided. It was now 12:21 a.m. and a young woman walking by herself at this hour (in Boston or any other city) was taking her life in her hands. Regardless, I attacked the garage now that it would shave ten minutes off my trip and shortly, I would be back in the relative safety of my apartment. How foolish could a country girl be.

Marc stood not less than three feet from me. He appeared out of nowhere. Wearing all black he blended in with the occasional lights and shadows.

"Hey, bitch, I told you I would catch up with you."

The anger in Marc's voice was compounded as it echoed off the garage's concrete walls. He sounded more demented than he ever had.

"What do you want from me Marc?, like I said, I didn't abandon you, I had no choice and about the police. If you hadn't attacked me on the street, they would have never been involved."

And just like that I ran. I knew he was going to kill me. I caught him flat-footed, he slipped while trying to catch up to me, giving me a bit of an advantage. It wasn't long however, before he caught up with me, now, grabbing me by my jacket as I tried to open an exit door in the garage. Before I knew it, we were struggling in the stairwell. He slapped me across my face. The sting resonated and incensed me even more, (if that was possible) and I think I surprised Marc with my strength, as I pushed him off me. He paused, taking a few steps back giving me just that one moment I needed to put my hand in my handbag, searching for my knife. The four inch steak knife was easily found. I secured its handle.

Marc surmised I was reaching into my purse to get something. He lunged at me again. I pulled the knife from my bag and stuck it in his eye. He took several steps back, covering his eye with his right hand, wailing in pain. I saw my chance, I could have run but I didn't. Attacking him I drove the steak knife deep into his chest. His cries resonated through the concrete tomb. Marc fell to the ground in a pool of blood, screaming in pain. I loved watching him suffer. I loved watching him suffer. *I loved watching him suffer*. I left him there to die. I walked home, took a shower and went to bed.

CAN YOU, HEAR ME NOW?

"**N**ora, can you hear me?"
He walked in front of me clicking his heels, snapping his fingers. I could barely hear him, every other click, a intermittent snap, then he faded out. I could hear him no longer. He fell off my radar screen.

My sonar picked him up again.

"Nora, do you know where you are?"

"*Yes, fuck head.*" I said to my self '*I'm in Boston, the home of the NEW ENGLAND PATRIOTS - and the beans - Boston Baked Beans.*"

"Nora, Nora, Nora, please pay attention to me."

I didn't feel like paying attention, to whoever he was, I didn't have a clue, not a one.

"Nora, please look at me."

I looked into his eyes. Whoever he was, escaped me."

"I'm Detective Karlsson, Viroqua P.D. and this gentleman standing beside me is Doctor Decker. He wants to ask you a few questions."

"Nora, I'm Doctor Decker, I'm from Madison and have traveled here to ask you as Detective Karlsson indicated, a few questions."

"Sure a few questions. I didn't know what he was asking but I would sure as hell answer what he wanted, to get whatever this was, over with, but I just wasn't sure, me being in Boston and all.

"Nora, again, do you know where you are?"

"Yes, I just answered that."

"Yeah, you did?"

"Yes, I did."

"Then, please answer it again."

"Like I said, I'm in Boston."

I didn't know why I had to repeat myself. I had already told the detective I was in Boston and I don't know why I had to tell them again. Why they were asking, I hadn't a clue - *the weirdest thing is that I hadn't a clue why I was where I was, not really knowing where I was at all. I started to question myself again: where the hell was I, and for what purpose was I here?*

"'You're not in Boston." Dr. Decker stated emphatically.

"Of course, I'm in Boston

"No Nora", the Doctor responded, 'No, you are not in Boston. You are in Viroqua."

I didn't know what game these guys were playing, but I left Viroqua several years ago and never looked back.

'No Nora, you think you might be in Boston but the truth is you never left Viroqua."

This was really bullshit. I don't know what yellow brick road these guys were taking me down but I damn well know sure it's leading nowhere because they are really very confused."

"Look, I don't really know who you guys are and what I'm doing here but you both have it all wrong."

"Nora', again, the Doctor responded, "This is why we are here, to determine who is right and who is wrong, to understand better what you are thinking."

"Again, I don't understand."

"You have an obsession with Boston Nora. You think you are living there but you are not. This obsession has taken you over. You have been doing nothing but pretending you are living somewhere you're not. Your parents saw this. They were seeing how you where living a pretend life, a life you weren't living, in the context of a person you are not."

I was beginning to get frightened. I still don't know what these guys were talking about but the reality is they were scaring the shit out of me. I needed to see my parents. I needed to speak to my siblings. I needed to speak to all of them."

"Yes, Nora. This obsession with Boston has been going on for quite some time. I understand your room is cluttered with everything pertaining to the city. You have wall to wall information and memorabilia, well not in your case, I mean something other than memorabilia. You have a great interest in the Boston Red Sox, the Boston Bruin's Hockey team, and especially the New England Patriots football team. Are you aware of that?"

"Of course I do, of course, I'm aware of that. I'm living in Boston, one of the greatest sports cities of all."

"But you're not Nora.."

"But I am, I replied.

"Nora, yes you have a deep-seated interest in Boston and its sports and a major one with bartending and mixing drinks. Your room is cluttered with information and it seems but a few years back, according to your friends, you had no interest at all."

I didn't really know what the doctor was saying. I listened out of politeness, knowing whatever he was speaking about would be quietly defused, once the detective and doctor spoke with my parents, sisters and brothers. I thought it in my best interest to get them here as quick as possible because I was still in a quandary as to what the hell was going on in my life. Was I in a rem sleep, caught up in a dream, or should I say a nightmare of some sorts. Whatever I was involved in was incredibly scary, bordering on the terrifying. I wanted my parents involved as quickly as possible. I need both my mother and father, brother, sisters, my friends to lead me from that which now I felt overwhelming.

I blurted out, "I want to see my parents."

"Your parents?"

"Yes, my parents, I do have parents."

I was now getting angry. I damn well know who my parents were and I know they know as well.

"Well?"

"Yes, my parents, I damn well need to see them."

Not a blessed sound, not a peep, not a snicker, nothing but a stare. Both men focused on each other. I saw their eyes meet. They both turned pale but not a word, not a damn one. Nothing, nothing, nothing.

"My parents, yes I want to see my parents and you need to get them here as soon as you can, or I am going to scream my bloody head off - I'm going to scream until I die."

I looked at the two men again and concluded either they didn't know where my parents were or they decided not to tell me. Either way, it infuriated me more with the absence of an explanation. Then the detective walked over to the doctor and whispered in his ear. I read his lips. He said, *"Do you think we should tell her?"* I screamed out, "Tell me what, tell me what? Damn it now. Tell me what?" The doctor, then turned his back on me and again whispered to the detective. This time I couldn't hear what he was saying. It was a brief discussion. Within seconds the doctor got up from his chair and walked towards me. He put his arm on my shoulder. I was pissed. I wanted to chew it off."

" Nora, my ass, what?"

"We need to discuss your parents."

"I don't want you to discuss them. I just want you to call them."

"We would if we could."

I was getting really upset. "It's easy Doc. You just call them and they'll be here as quickly as the sparrow flies."

The Doc answers with shaking of his head. "If only it was that easy."

I didn't know what was going on here. I'm confused, terribly confused and frustrated. In fact, I can feel the perspiration swelling up and soaking my armpits. I didn't know what was going on here. One minute I was in Boston, preparing to go tend bar at the The Crab Shack, and the next, here I am, - in Boston - in Viraqua - in Viraqua - in Boston. *Whatever!*

"So?' The Doctor asked.

"So, what the hell?" I replied.

The Doctor had a distant look.

"Yes, about your parents."

"Yes, what about them?"

The doctor in a confused look.

"You tell me you don't know?"

"Know what?"

"Your parents, they're dead!"

"DEAD?"

"Yes, - **DEAD**!"

YOU HAVE TO BE KIDDING

It was a lovely day in Viroqua, a canopied azure sky, temperature in the mid fifties, melting away the last remnant snow, bringing hope that summer would soon arrive.

I was asked to participate in another meeting at the Police Station, something about my family and me. I had no idea.

I left my cell accompanied by Lieutenant Miller. I liked him, he had a kind face with light hazel eyes and spoke in a soft comforting voice. He said this meeting was important and that finally all the pieces have come together (that's all he could say, he said he couldn't say anymore).

I walked into the interrogation room, the Lieutenant asked if I wanted a cup of coffee or tea. I declined. "But a glass of water would be nice," I said.

Lieutenant Miller and I sat at a long walnut table. It seemed much too large for two people. A few minutes later, we were joined by Detective Karlsson and another police officer, a rather large rotund man, bald, with a hard chiseled face.

"Can you hear me alright, Nora?" asked Detective Karlsson.

"I can hear you clear", I replied. "Why do you ask?"

"Cause yesterday, it seemed I didn't make myself clear or you quite didn't understand what I was saying, so we'll try again today, O,k?"

"O'k." I replied, not that I wasn't getting more confused by the minute.

"Well then , here goes."

Detective Karlsson refocuses, "Where's Decker?"

As if staged, Dr Decker, knocks on the door and enters the room.

"Sorry, I'm late, I wish I could say I was held up in traffic but this is Viroqua, there is no traffic."

We all smile.

"Well, please join us, Dr. Decker, we've just got started."

Karlsson again, introduces, the doctor to me and I greet him in turn.

"You're a doctor, but of what?" I asked.

"Psychiatry, I responded."

I thought to myself, Psychiatry, what the fuck? Lieutenant Karlsson, begins.

"Do you know why you're here Nora?"

"Honestly, haven't a clue, other than you coming for me and this ridiculous thing that my parents being dead."

"Nora, again, do you know where you are?"

"Of course I know where I am, being in Boston and all."

I see the three men looking at each other. I feel I'm the center of attraction. It's very unsettling and yet I still don't know why."

Dr. Decker interrupts, "Lieutenant, let me take it from here." Dr. Decker pulls his chair closer to the desk and me.

"Nora, in Boston, you are now in Boston, Are you sure?"

"I answered that. Yes, Boston, you know, Tom Brady and The New England Patriots. You know Boston Beans and such."

"Yes, that Boston, that's the one, but you're not. You are in your hometown Viroqua and you are now sitting in the interrogation room of the Viroqua Police Department.

Unnerved, "I really don't know what you are saying but you have it all wrong.

Dr. Decker continues. "This is why we are all here, to determine, who is right and who is wrong, to better understand what you are thinking, so with this in mind, you need to know you are not in Boston, in fact , In fact, you've never been to Boston. You living in Boston and the life you experienced are imagined.

I can't believe the nonsense you're saying, "No, no, you're wrong. I live in Boston and have been for several years now, and worked in a number of restaurants and bars, and had lots of boyfriends," I started crying, Lieutenant Karlsson hands me a tissue, and unfortunately had to kill the one who stalked me and tried to harm me.

Dr. Decker again, resolute, "Please hear me out Nora, there is no Boston for you, no restaurants, bars, boyfriends and none you murdered. You have to listen to me Nora, all this you are recalling is imagined. You are living another life. It is called Schizophrenic Histrionic mental disorder and for the people who have it. It's as real as it gets."

"You're all wrong. Then how do I know all this stuff about Boston and all the Boston stuff I have where did that come from? I mean like the Tom Brady #12 game jersey I'm wearing. Like where did it come from. I mean I didn't make this stuff up. I mean look at me. I'm wearing it. Touch it, feel, it's damn real as it's gonn'a get."

Lieutenant Miller. "Somehow, some way, you gathered and hoarded all this stuff. You're bed room at home looks like a Boston shrine, you have layers and layers of stuff on the floors and on the walls, Patriots, Bruins, Red Sox, and books about Boston and bartending, way too many to count."

"No. No. No. You're all mistaken. I don't know what you are trying to do to me but you are all wrong, *all WRONG!*

Karlsson continued, "Unfortunately not, and as far as your boyfriend Marc Mandady, you say you killed, it wasn't he you killed in Boston but rather your boyfriend Hans in Viroqua, whose head you split wide open with your father's antique Viking sword."

I sat, listening to him, paralyzed.

"You see Nora, after your parents and siblings were killed in their van returning home from the country fair in Madison, you lost sight of your reality and attacked and killed your boyfriend Hans after he called off your relationship being he saw you getting more delusional day after day. You thought he rejected you and you blamed him for everything that went wrong in your life.

THE FORBIDDEN FORREST

I remember as a small child walking towards the dark deep woods. The forest, as dense and alluring was terribly frightening. My father used to tell his children never to walk into the forest alone. Just several hundred yards from my house, he said sometimes, the comfort of our backyard ended only to open up to the trees, scrubs and obstructions, mostly unknown that the forest held. I often went to bed, and if summer, fell to the rhythm of the "peepers" who willed their barking call incessantly through the night. Fall would find the forest, God's great palette to paint his colors, red, orange and crimson dominated, intermittently making way for a flash of light brown and gold. During the winter months, I could hear the icy wind attack the leafless trees, with such aggression and vigor, that occasionally one would fall with a big thump.

Forbidden to ever enter the forest alone, my imagination gave way to what would be on the other side, if I indeed traveled to its very conclusion. Would it be that pot of gold that was at the end of the rainbow which my father several times pointed to as it broke through the sky or the terrifying monster of darkness, cold and loneliness, a forest of such density and mass could hold. The forest was always a big mystery to me, especially since there were so many in Viroqua, several my family would frequent, not ten, twenty minutes or perhaps an hour away, that we found great fun and pleasure, roaming through, imbibing in the crisp fresh air, the virgin fallen snow. We cross-country skied, snow shoed, went ice fishing (if indeed there were a lake or pond) and had snowball fights until exhaustion. Upon our return home we would pass the forbidden forest, that although much like the one we just left, was different than all the others, perhaps it was that me and my siblings were forbidden to enter because, it's density could gulp us up and we would be lost to our parents forever. The proximity to our house was probably the reason it was forbidden. It was always, there tempting me, my brothers and sisters always, mysterious and constantly frightening.

I learned early in life there are good forests and bad and no matter which they are, they had to be traveled, sometimes with others and sometimes alone. I now found myself at the end of my forest and it was deep, black vastness, not a light or glimmer to illuminate my way, just the dreadful deaf darkness that all people dread. I opened my eyes.

"DEAD" - what do you mean my parents are DEAD?"

"As you were told several weeks back, your parents and as terrible as it seems, your four siblings were killed in a five car accident on their returning from the county fair."

I couldn't believe what I was hearing. It was beyond my comprehension. IT CAN"T BE REAL - whoever this doctor is, is lying - why he is lying to me, I'll never know but he is, and to what purpose it serves, I hadn't a clue, other then ripping my heart from my chest."

"YOU ARE LYING TO ME - and I hate you for it. You must be a messenger from hell - dropping this insanity

on me - AND TO WHAT PURPOSE DO I ASK?" The
doctor takes my hand and I pull it away. I couldn't tolerate him touching me. He was vile. I wanted to get away
from him as quickly as I could but I was caught up in
this small room with the doctor and the detectives in
front of me, and basically I had no where to go - BUT
WHY THE TORTURE - WHY THE ABUSE - WHY THE
DECEITFULNESS AND LIES. "Unfortunately, Miss Bergman, I wish we could stop here but we can't. We need
to ask you several more questions. We wish we did not
have to do this but hopefully you understand that we
have no choice?"

"NO, NO, NOOOOO!!!, I need to get away from
here."

I Looked at the doctor as he turned to the Detective and with a dismissal of his hand, he said, "Detective
Karlsson, we need to take a break here. Ms. Bergman
obviously is under a lot of duress. She needs some time
- YES IT IS QUITE CLEAR SHE NEEDS SOME TIME.

MY PARENTS, MY, MY SIBLINGS, MY BOYFRIEND, ALL DEAD

I felt I was running through the forest, scrabbling to make sense of it all. I was running as quickly as I could. My heart was pounding through my chest. I stopped several times to catch my breath but as hard as I tried, I found it escaping me. My heart was heavy, burdened by the lack of air. I found myself steadfast, up to my knees in snow, unable to move. My feet were being sucked deeper into the dark, chilling wood and now I was up to my waist, and I could feel the power of the suction pulling me down. I frantically moved my arms, as a swimmer would against the tide and managed to, through divine intervention (it had to be divine intervention because it could not have been me alone) pull myself free.

It was indeed, minutes, hours, months, years, that I found my path and crawled, dragged and clawed my way to the opening when the sunshine should have been, where the forest ended. There was no sunshine, no light, not a glimmer but rather just the darkness that consumed me and now I realized that what was at the end of the forbidden forest, was probably the end of me.

www.ingramcontent.com/pod-product-compliance
Lightning Source LLC
Chambersburg PA
CBHW031309120626
46554CB00001BA/345